VIOLET SKY
FORBIDDEN LOVE

VIOLET SKY FORBIDDEN LOVE

EVE MARIAN

Paige Publishing

The characters and events portrayed in this book are fictitious. Any similarity to real persons, living or dead, is coincidental and not intended by the author.

Designations used by companies to distinguish their products are often claimed as trademarks. All brand names and product names used in this book and on its cover are trade names, service marks, trademarks and registered trademarks of their respective owners. The publishers and the book are not associated with any product or vendor mentioned in this book. None of the companies referenced within the book have endorsed the book.

ISBN-eBook: 978-1-7778-01304
ISBN-paperback: 978-1-7778-01311
ISBN-hardcover: 978-1-7778-01328

To my husband, Antonio,
who casually slipped my book into every one of his conversations.
His love and support inspires all my romances.

One

Hunter

My instincts begged me to kill him. I closed my eyes and took a deep breath to calm the anger raging inside me. When I opened them, the bastard with greasy blond hair stood about a hundred feet away with a smug smile on his face, but he wasn't smiling at me. He smiled at the woman in front of him, and satisfaction glowed in his eyes. She didn't smile back. Instead, she glared at him with her hands curled into fists at her sides. The bastard sneered but she didn't move.

We'd managed to get here in time—this time. We hadn't been so lucky in our last three attempts. In those cases, he got away before we could catch him. That would not happen tonight.

"John, go right and block First Street so he can't escape from there," I said, pointing John in the right direction. "Thomas, you take Main and make sure you block that route. I'll go straight for him and if he makes a move, we all pounce." I examined their faces, ensuring they understood. "I am not taking any chances. I don't care if the woman sees how fast we move. She probably won't realize what's happened until we're gone."

"Got it, Hunter. I'll wait for your signal," said Thomas, and we all moved into position.

I stepped toward the predator as slowly and quietly as I could, but he shifted his gaze in my direction. His nostrils flared and he turned to take one last look at the woman before he fled. His keen senses were probably the reason he'd evaded us so many times before. But tonight, we were prepared. Without hesitation, the three of us jumped on him before he could escape and then bound his wrists and ankles. I avoided his teeth and fingernails, which could expel venom. Even though the same venom ran through my veins, it would hurt, nonetheless. We carried him to a car waiting nearby. It all took less than five seconds, and then we were gone.

His name was Henry Jenkins, but I only saw a predator when I looked at him. John and Thomas shoved him into the back seat of the car. I was about to get in myself when a nagging feeling stopped me.

"Wait here, I'll be right back," I said to John, who ushered Tony out of the driver's seat. John always insisted on driving.

No one questioned where I went—they knew better than that. I found myself heading back to the alleyway to check on the woman.

She knelt on the ground, clutching the front of her blouse, her eyes searching the shadows around her. She whimpered. I stepped forward to offer my assistance but then hesitated. Her body shook, and she released the blouse to clutch her upper arms instead. I didn't need my predatory instincts to tell me she wouldn't welcome a strange man right now. Also, in her state, her senses would be in overdrive, and I didn't want to give her the opportunity to look too closely at what I was. I looked closer at her, though.

Her wavy red hair was tangled and it covered her face. Her body convulsed and she bent forward. She was in shock, understandably. She'd been fighting for her life one moment, then her attacker had vanished the next. She spied her purse a few feet away from where she knelt and crawled across the pavement to grab it. She rummaged inside until she found her phone. She dialed a number but shook the phone in frustration when no one answered. She tried again and this time someone must've picked up because she released a shaky breath and managed to keep her composure while speaking. Reassured that she had called for help and someone would arrive soon, I turned and walked back to the car.

"Tony, head back to the alleyway and keep an eye on the woman. Make sure she gets home. We don't know what else is lurking out there tonight," I said. Tony didn't say anything but he nodded, put his hands in his pockets and walked back into the dark alley.

I sat myself down next to Jenkins. I took his measure. He wasn't much to look at. Up close, his blond hair looked even greasier and his face sweatier. His skin had craters and was unshaven. He did not return my stare; instead, he looked forward. His hands shook. *Good, he should be scared.*

He didn't say a word and neither did I.

He knew where we were headed and what would happen to him there. We both knew the rules of our world and the consequences of breaking them.

As we approached Central Park, my cell phone rang. I recognized my sister's number.

"Hi, Laura," I said and hesitated, knowing the call would not go well.

"Hunter, where are you? I expected you at seven for dinner but it's 7:30 now." Laura produced indie movies, but she would have made an excellent army general.

She was in Toronto, debuting one of her documentaries at the film festival there. No one wanted to make this particular film—they'd said it wouldn't earn any money—but Laura had backed it financially and made sure the story was told.

"I got held up. I'll tell you about it when you're alone," I said, hearing the crowd around her.

"Are you still in New York?" she asked quietly, but her softness didn't fool me. I had a packed bag in my trunk and was on my way to the airport when I'd got a call from Thomas that he had eyes on Jenkins, so I turned the car around.

"Laura, I don't think I'm going to make it tonight. I'm really sorry, but..."

"What?" Laura said louder this time, and I knew in less than three seconds she'd remind me of all the business launches she'd attended on my behalf. She would be right, there were many, and she was there every single time.

Shit. I looked at the ceiling and released a breath before disappointing her, when I heard Thomas say, "Go to Toronto. We can drop you off at the airport and then take Jenkins to your father."

When I said nothing, he continued. "It's fine. We can handle it for you. The hard part is done. Go and be with your sister."

Thomas, my best friend, has always had a thing for Laura—even though she's too stubborn to see it. Of course, he would be the only one who'd feel worse than me for upsetting her. *Are you sure?* I mouthed to him. He nodded once and I knew he would take care of everything from here.

"Yes, it looks like the flight is delayed so I won't make dinner, but I'll be there for the after-party. Which one are you going to again?"

"It's the Hugo Boss party. It will be at Renegade nightclub on King Street."

I punched the details into my phone. "Okay perfect, I'll meet you there by ten."

"Great." Laura sounded relieved. "When you get here, you can tell me all about the bastard you finally caught." And she hung up the phone.

I turned to Thomas, who now had a guilty look on his face. He must have called Laura right after he'd talked to me. I shook my head and couldn't help but crack a smile. I may be the next in line to rule our kingdom, but Thomas would always fear disappointing Laura more than me.

"Hunter," Thomas began, but I raised my hand to cut him off.

"Drop me off at the airport and then take Jenkins to my father."

I took pity on Thomas. "I know how convincing Laura can be when she wants something."

I knew it well. One phone call from Laura and I was on my way to the airport again, headed for a Hugo Boss party in Toronto.

Michaela

My instincts tempted me to kill it—kill the music. I envisioned crushing the tiny speakers until they were crumbs on Emily's desk. The vision made me smile but then the music got louder, and I cringed. I decided on a compromise instead.

"Do you mind turning that down?" I asked over my shoulder and returned to staring at my nearly blank screen. My desk was not inside a typical cubicle. Instead, our boss, Suzanne Werther, thought we would be more creative and collaborative if we all worked in a large room together with no separations. She, however, had kept her office.

I couldn't see my coworkers' faces because my chair was turned away from them, but I imagined their eyebrows shooting up and their mouths pouting behind my back. I thought I heard someone whisper, "Did she skip her coffee this morning?"

Money was tight lately, but I always bought my morning coffee. My roommate moved out two months ago and the landlord had raised the rent this month. I was all on my own again. My car had broken down weeks ago and I still needed to come up with the funds to fix it. I had to take the subway to work and it was delayed. So, while I rarely skipped my morning coffee, today was one of those unfortunate days. I eyed the tiny speakers and planned their murder all over again.

I shook the image from my mind and returned my focus to my computer screen. I had ten minutes to book a press tour for a client.

If I didn't finish the itinerary soon, I would have nothing to show Suzanne for our ten o'clock catch-up.

"Hey, Mickey, are you coming to the Hugo Boss party tonight?" asked Tricia.

Tricia Sullivan was an account manager at Sway PR where I worked. She'd been hired less than a year ago but had already been given the title of account manager. It had taken me more than three years to get that title. So, I'd asked Suzanne to promote me to senior account manager, and she'd agreed. I was pleased but soon discovered that Tricia wasn't. Shortly afterward, Tricia started calling me Mickey.

She knew I hated it when she shortened my name, but whenever I reminded her that I didn't like it, she insisted it was a term of endearment.

"Yeah, I'll be there," I said, still staring at my screen. "Do you know if the Four Seasons lobby bar takes reservations?" I asked her while typing the hotel's web address.

"No, they don't," said Tricia.

I hit the backspace key and typed the Shangri-la Hotel instead. The website showed they took reservations. I reached for the phone to call the concierge.

"Hi, this is Michaela Morrone. I'd like to make a reservation...Yes, I'll hold," I said with a sigh.

"I will be at a client event but will come straight to the Hugo Boss party after I'm done," Tricia said.

"Sounds good. Do you need help at the event?" I asked.

"No, I'm good. I have it all under control," she snapped.

With the Shangri-la booked, I updated my itinerary and looked down at my screen. It was 9:58 a.m. I printed the itinerary and rushed over to Suzanne's office.

I slowed my steps when I was a few feet away. I lightly knocked on the door and walked in. Suzanne was on the phone, so she glanced at me and held up her index finger. I took a seat in front of her desk and waited.

When she hung up the phone, she turned and stared directly at me.

"What have you got for the press tour?"

I passed her a copy of the itinerary and showed her what I'd put together so far. She nodded as I went along. When I reached the afternoon meetings, she said, "Why book the Shangri-la if the Four Seasons is just down the street?

"Well...the Four Seasons doesn't take reservations. I didn't want to risk not having a table when we arrived," I explained.

"Of course, the Four Seasons takes reservations," she said. "Everyone knows that or a quick internet search would tell you."

The nerve of Tricia! I hadn't bothered to look it up when I'd asked her the question.

"No problem," I said, "I'll change the two o'clock meeting to the Four Seasons."

"Good. And make sure the editors attend the meetings, not the interns."

I nodded and made a note on my notepad. I always brought one. If Suzanne went on a tangent about another client, I didn't dare ask her to repeat herself. "Will do. Is there anything else you want to discuss?"

"No, that's it. Will you ask Tricia to come in?"

"Yes, of course."

I walked out of her office and back to our communal workspace. I tapped Tricia on the shoulder. She had her earphones in. I wasn't sure if she wore them to be polite or enjoyed that we went out of our way to get her attention.

"Hey, Suzanne wants to see you in her office." I hid my happiness when she looked at me with concern in her eyes. I didn't reassure her, instead I let her squirm and returned to my computer.

The next few hours went by in no time at all, with nearly everyone at Tricia's client event and me at my desk, blessedly, all by myself. It was now seven o'clock and I still hadn't finished booking the press tour. I decided to shut it down or I wouldn't make the Hugo Boss party. The event was the biggest after-party held at TIFF, the Toronto International Film Festival. Our office usually got VIP passes, but this year, I'd signed up one of my clients as a major sponsor, as well.

I peeked down the hall to the production room and spied Dev typing away at his computer. I grabbed my purse and walked over to his desk.

"Hey, time to pack it up and get going to the Hugo Boss party," I said.

"Ah, I don't know if I'm going," Dev said. "I don't like those sorts of things."

"What sort is that? Fun things?" I teased him. Dev was my best friend and an introvert. I guess opposites do attract. While he worked at a PR firm, he didn't like to work directly with clients. He took care of ordering all our promotional materials and putting together our press kits. He was a genius when it came to tissue paper and ribbon.

"You know I hate those events," he explained. "The ones where everyone looks around for someone better to talk to or is waiting for a celebrity to walk through the door. It's frustrating speaking to the side of someone's face."

He wasn't wrong. That's exactly what happened at these parties. Everyone's eyes looked a bit past you. Usually—in my case since I'm on the shorter side of 5'4—it was above me. While it annoyed me too, I still loved meeting new people and dancing with Dev. He always danced with me, despite his initial protests; he enjoyed it too.

"I promise to stick by your side the entire time. I won't let you out of my sight—I solemnly swear."

"That's what you said for that movie premiere, and you were gone for forty minutes," he reminded me.

I remembered that night and smiled. "All right that didn't count. Ryan Gosling was telling me a story. When he got that look in his eyes, I couldn't turn away. He trapped me there."

"Yes, and I was stuck talking to some manager," said Dev. "Who had an extraordinary ability to speak to me and the other person on his cell phone at the same time."

"That bad, huh?" I cringed when he nodded.

"That bad," he said.

"Don't worry. Ryan, or any other sexy celebrity, will not distract me tonight. I promise."

Dev's resolve gave in. A smile creeped up on his face. Despite his fear, he loved all the attention to detail and the payoff at the party. The custom napkins, the branded cookies, the swag bags...well, we all loved the swag bags.

"All right, but you can't leave me," he said as he pointed his finger at me.

"I won't, I promise," I said and crossed my heart. I would never leave Dev; he was all I had left.

Dev shook his head but shut down his computer. He pulled out his phone and called a cab to take us to the Hugo Boss party.

"Let's go," he said. "Before they run out of swag bags."

Two

Michaela

The lineup to get inside the Hugo Boss party wrapped around the block. Dev looked at me like he was about to bail, but I smiled and tugged him along. One of my favorite perks of working in PR was that I never had to wait in line to get into the parties we attended. We walked past the crowd and even past the bouncer.

"Where are we going?" asked Dev.

"We're going to the cast party," I said. "This one is upstairs and is exclusive to the cast and their people. Tonight, we are one of their people."

I gave him one of my best haughty smirks and raised an eyebrow for good measure. He laughed and straightened his collar as we left the crowd behind us.

I led us into the back alleyway toward a separate entrance. Tiny, who was well over six feet tall, stood with his arms crossed at the door. I'd met him yesterday when I set up the logos on the bathroom mirrors and checked that the banners were in all the right places. I'd had this great idea to plaster our client's logo on the mirror behind the bar. I knew everyone would be at the bar at some point in the night, but it wasn't easy to get back there. Tiny had lifted me onto the counter as I'd balanced on the edge with a credit card in one hand and the logo in the other.

"Hey, Tiny," I said and leaned in to give him a hug.

"Hey, shorty," he called back and flashed me his million-dollar smile.

"Our names should be on the list, Michaela Morrone and Dev Singh," I said.

He checked our names off the list and opened the door for us. "Everyone here?" I asked before going in.

"It's a good turnout, but a couple of the celebs still aren't here."

I wasn't surprised. The big celebrities often didn't arrive until much later and usually sat at a table in the corner, so they wouldn't be disturbed. But it was important that they showed—even if it was only to take a photo in front of the step-and-repeat banner at the entrance with all the sponsors' logos.

As we made our way down the narrow hallway, I congratulated myself for checking the venue yesterday. I wanted to look confident, and I couldn't do that if I was lost. I maneuvered us through the dark passageway and up a tight staircase to the second level.

The room was beautiful and opulent. The walls were painted a deep red and the sconces offered a warm light. Low-hanging crystal chandeliers hung throughout the space elevated the nightclub to a ballroom. A thick carpet covered the floors, except in the middle where a glass bar stood with two bartenders working furiously to keep the drinks flowing. Off to the left, a balcony overlooked a perfect view of the dance floor below. Clusters of white leather couches and small tables were scattered throughout, and most of them had already been claimed. Suzanne sat at one with the film's director and one of the producers.

"We should go say hi," I grabbed Dev's hand and walked over.

"Hi, Suzanne," I said, and gave a little wave in case she didn't hear me over the music.

Suzanne turned and beamed at me with her veneered smile. I couldn't help but smile back. She must be pleased with how everything looked. I sighed with relief. All those hours lugging boxes up and down that narrow staircase had been worth it.

"Hi, Michaela! Hi, Dev! Good to see you. Doesn't this place look great?" she said. I was about to say yes and thank her for saying so when she added, "Tricia outdid herself this time. I love that logo behind the bar downstairs she pointed out. It's brilliant. I don't know what I'd do without her. She's been a great addition to the team, don't you think?"

My mouth opened and closed like a fish, but nothing came out. Dev gently stepped on my toe, and I managed to spit out, "Yes, yes I don't know what we'd do."

"Well, go on, have fun and make some connections. We need to get our company name out to as many people as possible. Go do your thing."

She waved us off and resumed speaking to the people around her.

"Why didn't you tell her it was your idea to put the logo behind the bar?" asked Dev.

"I couldn't get it out. What was I supposed to do, shout that Tricia is a liar and it was me? This isn't the place to get into it. I'll speak to Suzanne on Monday."

Dev raised his eyebrow because we both knew I would let it go by Monday.

I grabbed his hand and led him toward the staircase. "Come on. Let's go downstairs and dance. I have to work off this negative energy somehow and dancing is what I need right now."

"And a drink," he said.

"Yep, that too." I agreed.

Hunter

I had a hard time finding Laura in the crowded room at first. But my heightened sense of smell traced her perfume mixed with her personal scent to the back of the club. I placed my hand on a few shoulders to weave through the crammed bodies. I received a few annoyed looks and some appreciative stares as I walked by. I followed the scent until I spotted Laura seated on a white couch with an entourage around her. Our kind doesn't often attract people—it may be a survival instinct for humans—but Laura had a natural ability to get people's attention with her genuine interest in their story.

"Hello, Laura," I said while her back was to me.

"Hunter!" She jumped up from the couch and gave me a hug. "Thank you for coming," she said. "I'd like you to meet a few people." Laura introduced me to a fellow producer and the movie's director. She then made room on the couch next to her and we all settled into conversation.

A little while later, I decided it was time to get away from the industry talk and get a drink at the bar. "Can I get anyone anything?" I asked and stood up from the couch.

"Hunter, we have bottle service," said Laura and she flagged down the waitress.

The tall brunette, who only moments ago had slipped me her number when she bent over to set down drinks for some of the other guests, turned to me and said, "What can I do for you?" I had to admit it was a great attempt at a sultry voice.

"Thank you, sweetheart, but I want to stretch my legs and head to the bar myself."

"If you need anything, you know how to find me." She smiled and sauntered away. Ah yes, but if she knew the truth, she wouldn't want anything to do with me.

I felt restless and wondered how Thomas fared with the predator. I scanned the room searching for a distraction. There were plenty to be found. Low conversations hummed around me, but I tuned these out. Plenty of beautiful people filled the club—the movie industry attracted them. While nice to look at, they bored me rather quickly. There was little I hadn't seen or done. I leaned over the balcony and looked out onto the dance floor below, when a woman seized my attention.

Her long, curly brown hair framed her shoulders and pretty face. Her smile radiated through the room. It was genuine and stood out among the fake ones. She laughed and threw her arms up over her head. Her unabashed joy cracked a piece of my armor. I'd built it over the decades, fortifying myself from getting too close to any human. Truthfully, it hadn't been all that difficult. In the beginning, I'd chased every beautiful face I met, but after a few years of just flirting, I lost interest. As I got older, I understood my duty to marry another like me and continue the family line.

A sharp intake of breath through my nose ensured I was not mistaken. No, this woman was human. I could only track Laura's scent from here and no other creature. For the first time in decades, a human woman had captured my attention, and this was the only time it'd happened without her uttering a word.

She must have felt me staring because she looked up and her eyes met mine directly. She stopped dancing and her arms went still at her sides. She pushed a lock of curly hair behind her ear with her fingers and smiled at me. Surprisingly, I smiled back. Some guy grabbed her hips from behind and coaxed her to dance with him. She turned back looking for her friend. A growl rose from deep within my chest. I held it down, but barely. I fought to keep myself in check because I had this undeniable need to go down there and rip his arms off. I ran my tongue across my teeth. My incisors had not lengthened. I took a quick look at my fingernails but those, too, remained the same. I worried that the disdain I felt toward that man would not keep them hidden for much longer. The friend waved his approval and the woman continued to dance. But my chest still heaved from my unexpected reaction. Laura walked up to me and put a calming hand on my shoulder.

"Hey, is everything all right?" she asked.

She stood next to me, but I still stared at the dance floor. Her eyes followed mine and she glanced back at me.

"You do realize she's human, right?" Laura prodded.

I felt her eyes examining me, but I couldn't turn my gaze away from the woman on the dance floor.

"What's gotten into you?" asked Laura. "You look like you're going to rip someone's throat out."

No, just his arms.

She didn't realize how close to the truth she was. Every muscle in my body tensed and I was ready to pounce, but I held back. A bead of sweat trickled down my spine from the effort. The struggle must have been obvious to Laura. She gently put her hand on my cheek and redirected my focus to her face.

"Hey, look at me," she said and I did. "Why don't we get out of here and you can tell me what kept you from dinner tonight."

Now that I was no longer staring at the girl, I could control my instincts better. "Yeah, good idea. It's definitely been an unforgettable night." But even as I said it, I'd hoped I'd be able to forget about her.

Three

Michaela

I can't believe you're going to New York City!" Dev leaned over my desk and nearly drooled on my keyboard.

It had been only two days since the film festival, giving me little time to prepare for our next event. This one would be held at New York Fashion Week and Suzanne had chosen me to go. I'd already arranged for our beauty client, Revive, to handle all the hair and makeup backstage at the shows.

"I know," I said with a grin. "We got *Canadian Glamour*'s Vanessa Steele an exclusive backstage with Revive's beauty team."

It would be four days of late nights, early mornings, and crazy schedules, but all worth it because I was going to New York City! Something about New York called to my heart. I had never been but always wanted to go. Last year, Suzanne accompanied Gabriel Santos—Revive's general manager—to New York and would have gone again this year if she hadn't come down with the flu. I got the call early this morning to pack my bags and ready myself for the red eye to the airport. Tricia, however, was green with envy.

"I don't understand why *you* get to go to New York," Tricia complained. "You've never even been there. At least I could show the client around."

I shrugged. The truth was, the client was my account, so I was the logical choice. But Tricia didn't agree. "Well," Tricia muttered as I walked past her desk. "I hope you know what you're doing and don't take her to the wrong restaurant. This isn't Vanessa's first time going. You don't want to look like you know nothing about the trendy hot spots."

I didn't respond but her comment worried me. The restaurant Suzanne had booked shut down due to a kitchen fire and just cancelled all their reservations. I needed to make a new reservation quickly. I sat at my desk and wrote down the names of a few of the most popular restaurants I found online and even checked out a few celebrity Instagram pages for ideas. But when I called, they were all full. I'd have to try a few more later. I planned to arrive earlier and familiarize myself with the places on Suzanne's itinerary, so I didn't look lost or inept.

I'd booked a noon departure to New York, which only gave me an hour to pack and get to the airport. It would be tight but worth it. I would have almost eight hours to explore the city on my own.

***

"Taxi!" I yelled, but the yellow cab drove right past me.

So far, New York City was nothing like what I had dreamt it would be. When I'd landed, the airport looked like it had not been renovated since the '70s and smelled even worse. The queue to get a cab was at least an hour long and my hotel room was the size of my closet at home.

Standing in front of my hotel, I shook off my negativity and instead focused on what I needed to do. I had wanted to get the full New York experience by hailing a taxi, but that hadn't worked out. Three had already driven past me and the last one gave me the finger.

I pulled out Suzanne's itinerary and opened my Google Maps app. Up first, breakfast with Vanessa and Gabriel at our hotel's restaurant in the morning. From there we were to meet up with Revive's hairstyling team at the first venue. How would Vanessa feel about taking the subway, I wondered? An image popped up of Editor in Chief Vanessa Steele in her pristine white dress and expensive pumps and I quickly dismissed the thought. I would book a car service to get us around town. I pulled up the client's budget and thanked Suzanne for allowing a few hundred dollars for miscellaneous expenses. I would arrange a car service with the hotel's concierge later today.

A dull ache pounded against my temples. I needed coffee STAT. I thought I saw a Starbucks around the corner when I first arrived at the hotel, but I couldn't remember if I had to go right on this corner or left. I turned right, checking the map on my phone at the same time.

Ow!

Did I run into a wall? I opened my eyes and stared at a dark grey suit lapel and black shirt. Okay, not a wall but equally hard. I wiggled my nose to check if it was broken.

"I don't think there's any damage to it," said a deep voice from above.

I raised my head and looked up. Way up. A pair of amber eyes stared back at me. They bored into mine and I stood my ground. He didn't smile. Despite his seriousness, I didn't feel threatened. Strange, a look like his would normally leave me reeling backward. But I stayed planted on the spot. The man looked familiar, but I couldn't place him. I couldn't shake the feeling that I'd seen him before.

"Are you all right?" he asked.

"Um, yes, I'm okay. Sorry, did I hurt *you*?"

His lips turned up a bit, which could have been a smile, but it didn't reach his eyes.

"No, you didn't hurt me. I've had worse run-ins," he said.

I didn't know what to say next. He was the most attractive guy I'd ever run into both literally and figuratively. His long, dark eyelashes curled up to frame his light eyes. He had a straight, narrow nose and a beautiful, full mouth. His dark hair shimmered—I wasn't sure if it was naturally that shiny or if he used a product to get it that way.

Don't you dare ask, Michaela.

"Um, I'm looking for a Starbucks around here. Do you know where I can find one?" I asked instead.

"Yes. There's one half a block that way." He pointed in the direction I'd just walked from.

Of course, I picked the wrong turn.

"Thanks," I said and smiled despite my humiliation.

"No problem. Why don't I walk you there in case you get lost again?"

"I wasn't exactly lost. Just wasn't sure where I was going, that's all." He looked at me, his dark eyebrows pulled close together, and then shook his head like he was about to say something but changed his mind. "I'm Michaela by the way," I said and stuck out my hand.

He stared at it before he reached out and took it.

"I'm not from New York," I said and nearly didn't hear his response over the beating of my heart pounding in my ears. I looked down at our clasped hands.

"I'm Hunter. And you don't say." He pulled his hand away and motioned toward the sidewalk. "Shall we?"

I harrumphed at his tone but tried again when we started walking. "Are you from New York, Hunter?"

"Yes."

Talkative, aren't you? "Sorry I ran into you. I was checking my phone and didn't realize you were standing there."

Okay, I was rambling, but I couldn't help it. This guy had my tongue in knots and made me nervous whenever I looked up at him. There was something both attractive and intimidating about him. His lips kept their straight line and he mostly looked ahead. I sneaked a side glance to check if I'd got lipstick on his shirt. I recognized the designer pinstripes and realized his shirt probably cost more than my entire outfit. Fortunately, there was no mark on his shirt or jacket.

"You must be Canadian," he said without any prompting.

"I am, how did you know? Was it my accent?" I asked, impressed with his deduction.

"No, you apologized twice in as many minutes," he deadpanned.

"Oh." Yeah, I did. Well, I was only trying to be polite. Unlike him, who had barely spoken even though he'd offered to walk me to the coffee shop. *Well, he won't get any more effort from me.* He may be tall, dark, and handsome, but something about him signaled danger. A chill ran down my spine, but I shook it off. *It's only coffee. It's not like I'm going to spend the rest of my life with this guy.*

Hunter

Of all the women on God's green earth for me to run into, it had to be her. What was she doing here? This morning I'd woken up irritated, having dreamt of her again. The dream was always the same: she stared up at me with eager eyes and a smiling mouth and I would slowly lean down and take it. I'd resorted to taking cold showers to erase the memories of those dreams. Today, I walked to work and hoped the fresh air would calm me down. Then bam! There she was—in my arms—staring right up at me. It took all my self-control not to grab her and kiss her.

Every word I spoke was measured. I concentrated on taking shallow breaths, as to not inhale deep gulps of her intoxicating scent. I kept my mouth shut, but it was no use, it was as if her scent permeated through my skin. I knew she felt my intensity but I didn't know how to make her feel at ease.

I would get through this chance meeting, intended surely to torture or test me—I wasn't sure which. I should have turned her in the right direction and sent her on her way, but I couldn't let her go just yet. Instead, I walked with her to Starbucks. Once inside, I would only stay fifteen minutes, and then forget about her. No matter what it took.

"I'll have a Caramel Macchiato, decaf, with almond milk, extra hot and, oh, extra caramel please," Michaela said.

She looked expectantly up at me for my order. I turned to the girl at the register and ground out, "Espresso. Make it a double."

"So, what do you do?" Michaela asked, while we waited for our drinks.

"I'm a property developer. I buy real estate and develop industrial or commercial properties for lease."

"That sounds interesting. Is there any property still to be developed here in New York?"

"This is just where we are based. I have properties around the world."

Talking about work calmed me down. It was familiar, and I liked the work. When I wasn't chasing rogue predators, Durand Enterprise kept me busy and productive. "How about you?" I asked.

"I work at Sway PR," she replied. "I am a senior account manager. I'm based in Toronto and love it there but have to say I'm pretty excited to be in New York for the first time, even though it's only for four days." She ran her hands through her hair quickly and then squeezed them together in front of her.

Her excitement spilled over to me, and I couldn't help but smile. She returned it with a big smile of her own. And just like that, I felt untethered.

"I think our drinks are ready," I said, even though no one called either of our names. I walked over to the barista and, God bless him, he brought my coffee to the counter.

"Michael?" called out a different barista.

"It's Michaela. Thanks!" Michaela reached over to grab her coffee.

Her sandalwood scent overwhelmed my senses. I closed my eyes and waited for it to pass. I should have ordered a triple.

I found two seats by the open window and pulled out a chair for her.

"Thank you," she said as she sat down, a blush rising on her cheeks.

Has no one ever pulled out a chair for her before? Chivalry truly is dead.

I let my hand rest on the chair so that her shoulder gently brushed it. It was barely a touch, but the spark of it nearly burned me.

I took a seat and tried to avoid eye contact but she had the most incredible eyes. They were a deep blue—no, they were purple with...were those golden specks? I'd never seen anything like them before. She had flawless, satin-like skin. I couldn't even detect a beauty mark from her neck down to her decolletage.

"So, maybe you can help me with something, Hunter."

"Sure, what can I do for you?" I asked.

"Well, I need to know which are the trendy restaurants. I need to book something for my client and an editor for tomorrow night. Any suggestions would be greatly appreciated."

"You need a restaurant reservation for tomorrow night? In Manhattan?"

Is she kidding?

"You need at least three weeks, sometimes more, to book a reservation in one of the top spots," I explained.

"I know. But the restaurant we had booked cancelled our reservation because of a kitchen fire and now I'm left scrambling," she groaned. "If I don't find something, this will be the last time I'll host a big trip like this." Worry clouded her eyes. An unnatural instinct to help her roared to life. *Those eyes will be the death of me.*

"One of my properties has a world-renowned restaurant, Savor,"

I said. "I know the chef and he always has a table or two reserved for me. I have plans myself tomorrow night to be there, but you can have the other table. It's near Sixth and West Fifty-Seventh street."

"Oh, my goodness, thank you so much! That location works perfectly." She placed her hand over her heart. "I don't know how to thank you enough. If there's anything I can do for you, please just let me know."

Stay away.

Afraid I would offer her something more than a dinner reservation, I decided my fifteen minutes were up. I excused myself with some explanation about being late for work and left her with her complicated coffee and a huge smile on her face.

That smile made me doubt myself. I'd never had any difficulty sticking to the rules before I met her.

Four

Hunter

The sommelier at Savor poured a glass for me to taste the cabernet sauvignon I'd ordered. I swirled it around a few times before I tried it. I didn't need to bring the glass closer to my nose, I could smell its rich aroma from arm's length. It was my favorite vintage, and the first taste soothed my anger as Thomas continued his story.

He was bringing me up to speed with everything I'd missed while away in Toronto. I was gone for barely two days, but it seemed I had missed a lot. They'd brought the predator before my father. There was no judge and jury for us—there was only my father, King Marsel Durand, our ruler. Magistrates around the world kept an eye on our kind in their own country, but the laws were written and upheld by the king. He decided which punishment fit the crime and his word was final. My father had been our king for more than two hundred years.

"Your father was indeed pleased when we brought Jenkins in," said Thomas. "He told us to put him in a holding cell until he decides what the punishment should be. He said he wanted to consider punishments meted out in the past and how he should deal with violence in the future. The problem began when your aunt Elenora demanded Jenkins be executed immediately."

My head shook involuntarily. My father's sister Elenora had questioned for some time now whether my father was strong enough to lead our kind and deter any rogues. Elenora would've been queen if she'd been born two minutes earlier. As her twin, my father gave her a great deal of authority in the kingdom, but it was never enough for Elenora. For years, I'd kept my eye on her, even though my father said she was all growl and no bite. But I didn't trust her. Or her son, Leo.

"That's when Elenora shouted, 'There should be no mercy to those who disobey our rules. Disobedience leads to chaos and chaos to anarchy,'" Thomas bellowed and he pounded the table with his fist. I worried his voice would carry so I shushed him. Chastised but not deterred, he continued in a whisper. "Your father was having none of her show of strength and responded, 'Mercy is not yours to give but mine, just like all the decisions of this kingdom are mine. Do not presume to give commands to me, Elenora.'"

Thomas sat back with a frown on his face. "I'm not going to lie, it was tense for a moment there, Hunter," he said.

Yes, it sounded like Elenora had made quite a scene.

"If you ask me, your father should have executed Jenkins immediately," said John. John was my cousin, and Uncle Theodore's son. He sat across from me and next to Thomas.

"Any act of leniency only shows violent perpetrators can get away with not following the rules," he said. Apparently, not everyone disagreed with Elenora.

"I did not ask you, John," I flippantly responded. Thomas snickered but covered it with the backside of his hand. But John noticed and snapped his head to look at him.

"What do you think the king will do about Jenkins?" Thomas directed his question to me.

"I don't know what the punishment will be."

"What would you do?" asked John.

Before I could answer him, my cousin Leo walked into the restaurant and distracted me. He wore a grey suit and a red tie.

He shook hands with the maître d' and then walked straight to our table. "Gentlemen," he greeted us.

"Leo," I said.

"Welcome back, cousin. I heard you had pressing business that kept you from your role by the king's side." Leo didn't believe in small talk. He got to the point, and I appreciated that, even when it grated on my nerves.

"It was family business," I said.

"Am I not family, as well?" he countered.

I wouldn't have dignified that question with a response even if the group at the door hadn't diverted my attention. I knew it was her even before I saw her face or smelled her sandalwood fragrance. My spine tingled as though I prepared to pounce but there was no reason for it. She leaned forward to speak with the maître d'. I'd warned him earlier to be pleasant to her, explaining she was a special guest of mine. Following my instructions, he smiled, gave a slight bow, and ushered her to the table just in front of ours. As she approached, she noticed me and a smile spread across her face. It felt as though someone had turned up the lights in the restaurant.

From the corner of my eye, I noticed Leo following my gaze. He glanced at Michaela and then back at me.

"Well, this is interesting," he said.

"What is?" I asked without taking my gaze off of her.

"Hunter taken in by a human girl."

"I don't know what you're talking about." I should have said nothing more. Instead, I went on. "Michaela is from out of town. She's here for Fashion Week and was desperate for a restaurant reservation, so I helped. That's it. There's nothing more than that."

"I think the gentleman doth protest too much."

I shot him a glare.

"So, you wouldn't mind if I go over and talk to her?" he continued with his aggravating accusations.

"Why would you want to do that?" I asked mildly, but my temper boiled under my cool exterior.

"Oh, I don't know. Pretty girl, not from here. She wants to be shown around, maybe shown a good time...."

The growl reverberated in my chest before I could stop it.

"That's what I thought," he whispered.

"Leo, you know the rules, I don't have to repeat them to you. You can't be with her."

Because she's mine.

I had no idea where that thought came from, but I shoved it back before I could think it again.

"Oh, I know the rules, cousin. I'm not going to break any of them, just maybe come a little close to bending them is all." And with a predatory smile, he walked over to Michaela's table.

The waiter had just taken their drink orders and handed them menus, when Leo arrived. I didn't need exceptional hearing to listen in on the conversation—Leo didn't try to keep his voice down anyway. "Michaela, is it?" he asked in that charming voice he reserved for making humans feel at ease.

Michaela's eyes looked at mine before she fully took Leo in. She had seen him approach from our table. "Yes. And you are?" she asked.

"Leonardo Durand," he said and stretched out his arm to shake her hand. But when she placed her tiny hand in his, instead of shaking it, he gently turned it and placed his lips to her knuckles. I resisted the urge to crack mine and instead opened and closed them into fists. "My cousin, Hunter, tells me you are from out of town and since he was able to help you with a dinner reservation, I thought I could help you with something, as well."

Michaela's brow creased, but she recovered quickly, smiled and looked around the table for a reaction from her guests. Everyone looked charmed by Leo, of course, and so she turned her attention back to him. "You want to help me?" she asked.

"Yes. Hunter tells me you are in town for Fashion Week."

"Yes, that's correct."

"Well, how would you like to meet with one of the designers?" And just as Michaela's eyes grew larger, Leo went in for the kill and said, "I can arrange for you all to personally meet with James Norton."

"James Norton?" she asked, astonished.

"James Norton!" gasped the other woman at the table. "I've been trying to interview him for years, but he hasn't granted an interview in more than a decade," she said.

That's because James Norton was one of us and had no need to give interviews or beg for attention. As one of my good friends, I knew James created because he loved it and didn't need to do anything else. This had also made him more elusive and sought-after than any other designer. It was quite an offer. But I didn't understand why Leo would go to all this effort. He would have to promise James something in return. All this just to annoy me?

I knew we had a rivalry between us, but this seemed like more effort than I would have given him credit for. I didn't know what he wanted but I did know this: I would be there with James tomorrow. There was no way I would let Leo get close to Michaela. If two predators lurked in a room with her, I would be there. Predators could never be trusted. I was not surprised when the entire table agreed to the meeting and they discussed details of when and where. Tomorrow. Four o'clock. Leo's penthouse on Fifth Avenue.

Having accomplished what he set out to do, Leo wished them a good evening and strolled back to our table with a grin on his face. "She has unusual eyes, your human girl," he said as he took a seat across from me.

"What are you up to?" I growled.

"Did you see how happy she was?" he said, putting his hands up.

"Answer. My. Question," I bit out. Leo's charming smile flattened into a straight line.

"James has done the recluse thing for too long. He needs to give a small interview before reporters start sniffing around for a different story. We have to do what we must to ensure no one ever suspects anything about us," said Leo. "You, cousin, should be the one worrying about our kind and not some girl."

"You're the one bringing her into this, not me," I said with controlled anger. "And James is not a problem, so you better make sure you're not creating one. In fact, I'll be there tomorrow to ensure it."

I felt Michaela's stare on us. I felt it the whole time I spoke to Leo, but I did not turn my gaze to look at her until that moment. Her eyes burned with unanswered questions.

She had said she'd be in town for only three days. I could keep it together until then. I had managed to control my instincts for more than a hundred years. *How hard could three days be?*

Five

Michaela

New York was everything I'd hoped it would be. I could live there forever. I'd chatted with Suzanne earlier. She felt better and threw herself back into work. She told me she'd spoken with Vanessa. They were both impressed that I'd managed to secure an interview with THE James Norton. Vanessa even planned to make it a cover story in her magazine.

I spied Vanessa Steele at the lobby bar. It was 3:25 p.m. and we were supposed to meet at the bar in five minutes and leave for Leo's penthouse.

Vanessa was early as usual, the consummate professional. She terrified me at first. She wasn't mean, but Vanessa didn't go out of her way to be nice either. She was curt in her replies and particular about the stories she wrote. She wrote to inform, even if some would say beauty trends were fluff. To her, they were as important as taking down a nefarious politician.

I once did a deskside product meeting with her for a new sunscreen and when the client displayed the three very pale color options on the boardroom table: ivory, beige and sunkissed, I knew she would nail them for not being more inclusive with their options. I loved her for it.

I crossed the lobby to greet Vanessa when I felt a hand on my arm. I turned to see Gabriel.

"Hello, Michaela," he said and directed me away from the lobby bar.

"Oh, hi Gabriel," I greeted him and took a step back.

"Listen, I want you to know I think you're doing a great job."

"Thank you."

"I'll admit I was worried when I heard she wasn't coming and sent her account manager instead, but I was wrong."

Senior account manager, but now was not the best time to correct him.

"I feel like we have this magic together, you and me."

I nodded, unsure what he meant by that.

"Why don't you drop me an email when you're back in the office. Let's book a time to chat. I'd like you to do some PR for us in the US. We've acquired a new account and I think you're the right person to handle it."

"I would love that. I'll drop you a line when we're back at the office."

"Perfect, now let's go meet this James Norton everyone's talking about."

***

The driver pulled up to the address Leo gave me at dinner last night. I tipped him and thanked him before following Gabriel and Vanessa out of the car.

A doorman greeted us at the entrance to a stunning foyer that looked like it had fallen out of some travel digest magazine. We walked toward the elevators, and I noticed a separate one for the penthouse suites. When the doors opened, I held them until Gabriel and Vanessa followed me inside. None of us had spoken yet. It all felt like a dream or reality TV show, and I didn't want to wake up or change the channel back to my ordinary life.

When the elevator doors opened, we walked out together like some fashion trio strutting down a carpeted runway. To my right,

Vanessa wore a white mid-length designer dress; to my left, Gabriel had on a perfectly fitted navy suit; and I wore a short black sweater-dress with four-inch heels. A Canadian designer had gifted me the dress when I'd partnered them with a lucrative sponsor.

I walked down that hallway like I was born for this.

I knocked on the penthouse door, stepped back and waited for someone to answer. The door opened and Leo stood there on the other side. He grinned from ear to ear.

"Michaela, welcome," he greeted us.

"Leo. Thank you for having us," I said.

"Please, come in. James will join us shortly. This is my cousin, Hunter. I know you two have met."

I followed Leo's outstretched arm toward the divan and saw Hunter get up slowly.

"Michaela," said Hunter with a nod.

"Hunter, hi. It's great to see you again," I said with a genuine smile, because despite his cool demeanor my body temperature spiked whenever he came near me.

"This is Gabriel Santos, Revive's general manager and this is Vanessa Steele, editor in chief of *Canadian Glamour* magazine," I said.

Hunter stepped forward to shake Vanessa's hand, then Gabriel's.

"Hunter is a big fan of beauty and fashion. He insisted on joining us today," said Leo, cutting Hunter a pointed glance. I thought I heard a growl from Hunter's direction but couldn't be sure.

"Come, let's sit down. Can I get you something to drink?" Leo asked.

"Scotch, if you have," said Gabriel.

"I'll take a Gin and Tonic," said Vanessa.

"Make that two, please," I replied.

"And you, Hunter?" said Leo. "Tell me, what is it that you want?"

The way he said it had me looking back and forth between the two of them.

Hunter didn't respond at first, but then said, "You know me, I'm an Old Fashion kind of guy."

I wouldn't have pegged him for this drink but he was full of surprises.

"Yes, I knew you were, but I thought that may have changed," Leo said while he prepared the drinks.

Hunter gave him a smile but it looked more like a grimace.

And then James Norton walked in. All eyes in the room turned toward the tall, slim, elegant man in a tailored and beautifully stitched grey suit.

"Hello," he said.

"Hi," the fashion trio managed in unison.

Leo stepped forward and began introductions with me first, then Gabriel and finally Vanessa. He seated Vanessa and Gabriel on the divan across from where James sat down.

James had a trace of a British accent, or perhaps more refined speech that came across like an accent to me. Either way, it intimidated me. But Vanessa did not seem thwarted. She pulled out her tape recorder and notepad and placed them on her lap.

I hovered in the background, close by if needed, but I didn't want to be one of those PR people that dictated an interview. I found that tactic usually upset journalists, and never resulted in a good story.

From the corner of my eye, I noticed Hunter coming my way. His walk was slow and measured, accentuating his strength rather than his swagger.

I hadn't been this close to him since the coffee shop, and it felt like all the air had been sucked out of the room. I tried to take a deep breath to calm my racing heart.

I didn't know why he had this effect on me. Yes, he was gorgeous, for sure. His broad shoulders seemed to block the sun whenever he stood near, making me want to close my eyes and snuggle into him. But, I had been around beautiful people before. In fact, I'd built my whole career around beauty. There was something different about him.

"Did you enjoy the restaurant last night?" Hunter asked when he stopped in front of me.

"Yes, the food was delicious, and the atmosphere was just as I imagined it would be. Thank you again for arranging that."

"It was my pleasure," he said with a smile. The way those words rumbled through his lips made me shiver.

"And thank you for asking Leo to arrange this interview. I cannot tell you how much this has helped me and my career," I said, trying to get back on track.

"I cannot take credit for that. This is all Leo's doing," he explained.

"Oh, I thought that's why you were here. That you asked him to arrange this. If that's not it, then why are you here?" I blurted out.

Hunter looked like he was about to say something but then paused.

"I'm sorry. That came out rather rudely. I didn't mean to sound like you shouldn't be here, just... I guess I was wondering why you came."

He still didn't speak for a few moments, looking around the room, and I scolded myself for ruining the conversation. He turned back to me and, finally, responded, "For you."

"Pardon?" I asked because I could not have heard him correctly.

"I came for you," he repeated. "I know we just met, but I feel drawn to you, and irrationally protective."

"Me?" I asked, with my hand to my heart and my eyes bulging out.

"Yes. You," he said with a smile. "When I heard you were going to be here, inside Leo's apartment with James, I needed to be here too, to make sure you would be all right."

"Why wouldn't I be all right?" I asked, shaking my head.

"Because...well...Leo can be very charming and James, too, in his way. I didn't want you to fall for one of those devils and return to Toronto heartbroken."

He smiled again and I couldn't help but smile back. I didn't believe what he'd just told me, but it was charming and there was no reason to be a bloodhound.

"Mmm. Well, thank you, I think. That's awfully sweet of Leo to help me out," I said. "I will have to properly thank him."

"You really don't need to do that," he said, his mouth twisting.

"So, if Leo is your cousin, how do you know James?" I asked.

"James is an old friend. He lost his parents when he was incredibly young, so he practically grew up with me. He was at our home quite often."

"Oh, that's terrible. I mean, about his parents," I said, my mind drifting toward memories of my own parents.

"Yes. He doesn't talk about it much," said Hunter.

"Neither do I." The words slipped out and I realized too late that I'd said too much.

"You lost your parents too?"

The concern in his eyes convinced me to speak more than usual. Normally, I would say it was a long time ago and leave it at that. Instead, I went on.

"Yes, when I was sixteen. My parents were researchers and travelled a lot. I remember them often rushing somewhere when I was young and leaving me with my aunt. I thought they were lucky, always off to a wonderful new adventure. I couldn't wait until I was old enough to join them."

The next part always choked me up. But I gathered up my courage and continued.

"Shortly after my sixteenth birthday, my parents went to Italy for another trip. It wasn't supposed to be long, only a week. But after the third day, they boarded a small plane...and...it went down somewhere in the Adriatic Sea."

I took a deep breath and let it out slowly.

"I'm so sorry, Michaela," Hunter whispered.

It was nearly ten years ago, but I still couldn't talk about it without feeling the same pain I felt back then. Utterly lost and alone. Time may heal the wound, but the scar will always remain.

He reached over and cradled my cheek. His thumb rubbed back and forth underneath my eye. I must have shed a tear because my cheek felt wet.

Hunter leaned in and kissed my eyelid. My eyes remained closed, but I felt his lips on my temple and then he softly kissed my cheek. He didn't move away and neither did I. His breath felt cool against my wet face but warm against my lips. I parted them and deeply inhaled the air between us. He groaned and then sealed his lips onto mine. His mouth was gentle and moved slowly. My head spun and I couldn't breathe.

I heard a gasp. At first, I thought it was mine, but I soon realized it came from the other side of the room. I jerked out of Hunter's embrace and saw four pairs of eyes on us, and a smug smile on Leo's face.

Six

Hunter

Dammit. I never meant to get that close to her and I definitely never meant to kiss her. But when tears fell down her face, I lost the reins on my control, and the animal inside me broke free. I could not stop myself from touching her, holding her—possessing her. Someone on the other side of the room gasped. I didn't know who. Regardless, it wasn't good. This was an important day for Michaela, and I had blown it for her.

"Ah, Hunter was helping me," Michaela stammered. "Um, I had something in my eye. I'll just go to the bathroom and rinse it out. Please, carry on." Vanessa tossed her hair back and asked James another question. Gabriel's gaze still lingered on Michaela.

Michaela pivoted and rushed out into the hallway.

"First door to the left," Leo called out. Amusement lingered on his face as he sauntered closer to me. "Something in her eye, huh? Looked like you were aiming a little lower," he said with a chuckle.

"This isn't funny, especially not for Michaela," I said. "I am the one to blame. I should do something."

"Oh, I'm sure it was your fault, but I think you've done enough." He laughed.

I glared at Leo with all the frustration and anger I felt at that moment. To his credit, he winced.

"Don't stare at me like that. It's hard to think of a plan to smooth things over when I'm looking for escape routes. Why did you do it?"

"Kiss her?" I asked, buying time.

"You have better control than that. At least I thought you did," he said.

"I don't know what happened. One minute, I'm asking her about dinner, the next she is telling me about her parents. When I saw the pain in her eyes, I couldn't think of anything else but comforting her."

I paced the room but stopped when James looked up at me. His raised eyebrow warned me before I caught any more unwanted attention. I ran my fingers through my hair in frustration instead.

"This is bad," said Leo.

"Don't you think I know that?" I growled.

Michaela walked back into the room a few minutes later. Her shoulders squared and a determined look spread across her face.

I felt gutted. I wanted to apologize but she spoke first.

"I have to do something to make Vanessa and Gabriel forget what they just saw," she whispered to me and Leo. Her voice was soft but crisp. "Something big that will eclipse a silly kiss."

I frowned. The kiss was not appropriate, but it definitely wasn't silly. It was a pretty great kiss, actually. I may have to do it again to prove it.

"Leo, do you think you can get James to provide *Canadian Glamour* with one of his latest gowns to use for their next cover shoot? It would be an exclusive before he launches," Michaela suggested. "*Canadian Glamour* would be the stage to unveil one of the statement pieces of the collection before it hits the runway."

Leo's eyes widened in appreciation before he said, "It would be quite the coup."

"Do you think he'll do it?" she asked him, her eyes beseeching.

Leo didn't stand a chance. He smiled at Michaela and then glanced at me. He looked just as impressed as I was with her quick thinking.

"That's a brilliant idea, Michaela," said Leo. "In fact, I'm surprised I didn't think of it myself. Leave it with me. James will do it," he assured her.

Again, I wondered what Leo had over James for him to be so accommodating. I made a mental note to speak to James about that.

"Perfect, thank you so much," Michaela said, her palms pressed together at her chest.

With that all sorted out, I turned Michaela away from Leo to apologize in private. "I'm sorry about the kiss," I said but then thought better of it. "Well, not sorry about kissing you, just that it was in front of your colleagues. I didn't mean to put you in that situation. That's not like me."

"I'm not sorry about the kiss either. Just the timing," she said with a smirk. Then she asked, "What are you doing tomorrow? I have a packed day of meetings but I'm free all night. It will be my last night in New York...maybe you could show me around."

I could show you the world, sweetheart. But I couldn't share it with you and that would be agony.

But if one night was all I had, I would keep it together and savor a few more hours with her. Knowing she was still in my city —I probably couldn't manage to stay away. So, I agreed.

"Absolutely," I said and smiled. "I'll pick you up at six."

She returned my smile with a bright grin of her own and a quick nod before moving closer to the couch as the interview wrapped up.

***

A short while later, Leo escorted Michaela and her guests into the hallway, and I walked over to the side tray to pour myself another drink.

"Can I get you one, James?" I asked.

James stood by the large balcony, looking lost in his thoughts.

"Yes, I think I need it. What the hell was that?" he asked.

I cringed as I poured two fingers of scotch into a tumbler.

"Ugh, don't mention it," I said. "I still feel bad. I didn't mean to kiss her in front of everyone. That was a lapse of judgement."

"I'm not talking about your timing. I'm talking about what that kiss caused—it was quite a stir," he continued.

"Yes, I heard the gasp too, James. Vanessa must have been surprised to see us kissing," I explained.

"I was the one who gasped," said James. "And I wasn't surprised by the kiss but by my body's reaction to it. My heart actually stopped."

"What are you talking about?" I asked, but my heart raced now. "You sound ridiculous." My flippant words did not match my emotions.

"I don't know what to say, other than, when you kissed her, my heart stopped beating for a few seconds before kicking up again. Did you not feel it here?" He said and placed a fist to his heart.

How could that happen to James?

When I didn't respond, James walked over and stared at me. His eyes searched mine, digging for an answer.

Yes, of course I felt it. But I'd kissed her—me. I'd held her in my arms. My heart stopped when I first saw her at TIFF and again when I'd kissed her just now. I'd never felt that before. But it didn't make sense that James would feel it too—twenty feet away.

"I don't understand what you're saying," I argued, shaking my head. None of this made any sense.

"Neither do I. I've never felt that before," he said, echoing my earlier thought. He resumed his pacing in front of the balcony. "But I definitely felt it. And it was strange."

Abruptly, he stopped pacing and sucked in a breath. When he turned toward me, his eyes grew larger by the second.

"You didn't break the first rule, did you? You didn't tell her what we are?" he asked, his voice barely a whisper.

"Are you serious, James?" I shouted, insulted he would even think it. "What would I even say to her? Hi, I'm Hunter. I'm the heir to the Manticore Kingdom. Oh, you don't know what a manticore is? Well, we have the predatory instincts of a lion, and the venom of a scorpion runs through our blood."

I raised my hand in front of my face, curled my fingers into a fist and sneered. "It means that when I get angry or my instincts take over, I can use my venomous fingernails and teeth to kill you."

I smiled but knew it looked more like a grimace. "Yes, I could kill you without much effort on my part. And if I can't control my instincts, I could kill you without even wanting to. Would you like to go for a drink after this?"

My nostrils flared and I breathed like a raging bull.

James stared at me, unimpressed with my tirade, and I stared back.

Leo walked back into the apartment and slapped me on the shoulder.

"Well, that went well, didn't it, Casanova?" he said with a Don Juan smile of his own.

I groaned. I would never live this down with Leo.

"Leo, did you feel something when Hunter kissed Michaela?" asked James.

"Feel something? Like the room getting colder because he sucked all the hot air out of it with his mouth?" Leo teased.

"No." James waved his hand like he could bat Leo's pesky teasing away. "Like something with your heart?"

"Probably not, because he doesn't have one," I sneered. I had lost my patience with Leo.

Leo looked at me like he would argue but instead shook his head. "No, I didn't feel anything like that. Why?"

"Because I did, and I've never felt anything like it before," explained James.

"Well, maybe you need to see someone because I felt nothing, and I don't know why I would," said Leo.

"I don't know either, but there's something going on," said James. "Did you notice her eyes?"

"Of course," I said.

"They are uncommon and yet I feel like I've seen them before," explained James. "Though, I can't remember where."

"Well, speaking of those pretty eyes, they have a request for you," said Leo, soldering up to James. "You are not going to like it, but I know you'll do it."

I didn't listen to the rest of what Leo and James discussed. I was preoccupied thinking of what James had said. He believed he had seen her eyes before. I scanned my memory, and something tickled in the back of my mind.

Where have I seen purple eyes like hers before?

I closed mine to recall, but I couldn't see anything but her.

Seven

Hunter

I spent the remainder of the day at the office but the only thing I managed to concentrate on were James's words. I tried over and over to recall any chance meeting or even a reference to someone with purple eyes but could not think of one. I was embarrassed to say it likely wasn't because I'd never met anyone else with purple eyes, only that I had never cared enough to notice. My work and family had always consumed me—until now.

I swiveled my office chair toward my computer and typed "purple eyes" into the search bar. Below, a few images of Elizabeth Taylor popped up and underneath those were several links referencing internet myths. The internet myths proved to be just fiction. I clicked on a few supposed medical links but each one claimed purple eyes at birth did not exist. Either Michaela wasn't born with those eyes or there was another explanation—one beyond the scope of online medicine.

I didn't find much else online, so I decided to head over to our kingdom's library. Perhaps there were books or notes there that explained purple eyes. Any real link between purple eyes and the supernatural would be recorded in our library.

I walked through my office parking lot toward my car—it was a little flashy, but I loved the way it drove. I stepped inside and started the engine. I easily merged into traffic and enjoyed the ride to Central Park. The skyscrapers ripped the skies, and the trees towered above the people. New York really was a beautiful city to drive through, when no one honked their horn at you and pedestrians didn't walk in front of your car.

This afternoon, the drive was a busy one to the parking garage located behind Central Park. A gate protected the private lot and only those of us with scanned passes could enter. I parked in my designated spot next to the elevators and walked briskly through the doors. I used a different access card for the elevators. I pressed it against the scanner and selected the basement button that lowered me to our underground kingdom. My ancestors had hidden our kingdom beneath Central Park, ensuring no one would dig and discover our ancient ways. While we did not live underground, our library, dungeons, courts, and crypts were hidden away there.

When the doors opened into the basement, two security guards stood by to greet any visitors or remove any unwelcomed guests who'd managed to get this far.

"Anthony. George," I said with a nod to each as I walked past them.

"Mr. Durand." They nodded back but continued to look straight ahead.

Long, narrow hallways constructed in brown stone distinguished this part of the kingdom. When I was young, I'd run up and down the hallways, opening each door to discover where it would lead me. Today, I took the hallway to my left that led to our library.

The room was more than six thousand square feet and was lined floor to ceiling with books, manuscripts, archives, and scriptures. I'd never bothered looking anything up on the computer—I always went directly to Ernest. He'd worked at the library for more years than I'd lived.

"Ernest. How are you today?" I said and reached out to shake his hand.

He returned my greeting with a jubilant smile. "Fine, Mr. Durand. How are you?" he said, bobbing his head up and down.

"I'm well, thanks. I'm looking for some information pertaining to purple eyes. Can you think of anything that would give me some insight into this genetic anomaly?"

"Mmm. Well, there are medical journals, of course."

"No, I'm not looking for the technical reason for purple eyes. Something different, something that may not be as obvious," I explained.

"Well, you can always check our books on folklore, fairies, and fantasy," he suggested.

"All right, I'll start there if you can point me in the right direction."

Ernest indicated a section to my right, in one of the farthest corners of the library.

"Thanks, I appreciate the help," I said.

"No problem. Anything else I can do, just let me know."

As I walked in that direction, I spotted a figure to my left in one of the private studies. The studies were all glass enclosures, visible but soundproof. In one of the rooms, I observed my father. Without giving it a second thought, I walked over.

He hunched over the desk. His hand rested on his forehead and a pile of books laid beside him. I hesitated for only a second but then knocked on the door anyway. He looked up and I hesitated again. I didn't want to interrupt him.

"Am I disturbing you?" I asked, poking my head through the door frame.

"Hunter, enter," he said as he waved me in. "I was looking over some previous cases. Comparing past judgements."

"And what have you found?" I asked.

"I've found instances where kings have executed manticores for less than what this one did and other instances where they were locked in the dungeons for murder. A little consistency would be appreciated," he said with a hint of a smile.

"What are you going to do?" I asked, surprised to discover I was as impatient as everyone else to know what he planned to do next.

"I really don't know," my father said with a sigh. "He broke our rules and attacked three humans. According to our laws, he should be executed. However, I have been working so hard to make changes within the realm. I want to show compassion and mercy and perhaps even rehabilitation."

"Do you think this offender can be rehabilitated?" I asked, none too convinced.

"I spoke to him yesterday," he said. "It's strange because he refuses to give me any background on himself, but he has admitted to all the assaults and flaunting his powers in front of humans. He begged for his life and said he would change if given a second chance."

My father took a breath and then said, "I swear a hundred years ago, I would have probably beheaded him on arrival, but today I feel we can go further with a new order of justice. I don't know, maybe I'm getting soft."

"No. You want us to be something more than monsters. And you've done it. During your rule we have assimilated to work, to live, and to interact with humans without detection for hundreds of years. I don't want to go back to living underground in sewers or caves like our ancestors before us did. They could not control their instincts. Under your guidance we have changed. Or at least most of us have," I said. "I don't know what the right decision is, but I know you will make it."

"Thank you, Hunter," he said and, as if he'd just realized where we were, he added, "What brings you to the library?"

"Oh," I said, a bit embarrassed to admit girl trouble had me running around the city. "I wanted to look into a particular rule about manticores and sports. I'm pretty sure I saw something about not competing at the Olympics, but professional sports are fair game."

"No, that's not correct. A manticore's speed and strength would definitely raise questions and potentially threaten our secret. Manticores should stay away from sports, except when it comes to building franchises. Then we manticores have a lot to offer. Besides, a few of the owners are manticores themselves."

"That makes sense," I said. "I'll just find the annotation in our library. I wouldn't want to get Aunt Elenora's tail in a knot over this."

He smiled at my joke, and I couldn't help but feel like a kid again.

"Good luck, Father. I know you'll do the right thing," I said, even though he didn't need my approval.

"Thank you, Hunter. I hope the decisions I make today will help you with yours in the future."

"Well, I'm in no rush for that future," I said and closed the door behind me.

I continued walking along the rows of books until I reached the folklore corner. I pulled out several books that interested me, including *Fairies Among Us*, *Folk Stories Untold*, *Lessons on Legends* and a few more for good measure.

I skimmed through the chapter titles, index pages and glossaries. I found an interesting chapter about the origins of The Faerie Queen. It said she was first referenced by English poet Edmund Spencer and then by William Shakespeare as The Fairy Queen in *A Midsummer Night's Dream*. However, her true origin was believed to be in Ireland. The next passage gave a brief description of the fairies.

Fairies like to stay very close to nature. They can be found living in forests and particularly like to play around water. They are immortal but cannot reproduce among themselves—a fairy can only be created by the Fairy Queen. This may explain their fascination with infants and children. They prefer to stay within their own dwellings, rarely venturing farther than their woods. They love to play tricks on humans and over the years have gotten a number of humans in a bit of trouble. There are very few instances of fairies living among humans. Fairies do not find human ways amusing and do not wish to live among them.

I put the book down on the table and my mind wandered to my own fairy experience. I had only met one fairy in my lifetime. It was in Dublin in 1926. I was out walking near the woods when a beautiful creature emerged from the trees wearing a white dress and white flowers in her dark hair. She had beautiful red lips, but her smile did not reach her eyes. Her hips swayed as she walked closer toward me, and she laid her hands on my chest.

"Hunter, my love, will you prove yourself to me?" she beseeched me in a musical voice.

"I'll do anything you ask," I remembered saying. Knowing I would agree to anything this creature asked of me.

"Go to the blacksmith's house and bring me his newest babe. I only want to hold him for a little while," she said, arranging her arms like a cradle, swinging an imaginary baby.

"Yes, I will do that for you," I responded. She leaned in and kissed me with her red lips. She tasted like a cold river on a hot day. It was as if I hadn't drank in days.

I found myself heading toward the blacksmith's house and knocking on his door. His wife answered with a newborn babe in her arms, sleeping peacefully.

"Yes, can I help you?" she asked, looking exhausted.

A dog barked from behind the woman, waking the baby. The tiny tot gave a screeching wail, fists outstretched in the air and legs shaking. The loud cry must have woken me up from a dream state. Confused, I could not understand why I would ask this woman to give me her baby.

"I'm sorry madam, I must have gotten the wrong house," I said.

Without giving me a second glance, she closed the door in my face. I thanked that dog in my thoughts over and over again for saving me and the baby. That fairy had more than mischief on her mind—I was sure of it.

I turned the page, wanting to move on from the memory. The next few chapters didn't seem to be relevant to what I was looking for. I reached for *Folk Stories Untold* and fanned out the book. My eyes caught a photo of an iris and I immediately put my thumb on the page to open the section. Staring back at me were a pair of violet eyes, very much like Michaela's.

Eyes of the Gods

Dear reader, this is a story told for thousands of years and yet it is relatively unknown. It takes place in ancient Egypt, among the pharaohs, the beasts, and the gods. There was a young and beautiful woman with raven black hair and purple eyes, but it was not her striking features that earned her the attention of the villagers around her; it was her song. She had a voice like that of a songbird and she sang wherever she went. Her voice would bring joy to the sorrowful, it would soothe the sick, and on rare occasions make your heart leap so high you could hardly breathe. Yes, she was that wonderful, that powerful. Her parents named her Violet, after the unusual color of her eyes that she'd inherited from her mother. But unlike her mother, who kept to herself, Violet wanted to share her gifts with others. She knew they were too special to keep secret. One day, as she made her way through her village to visit a friend sick in her bed, Violet came across a ferocious beast. The beast had long nails and sharp fangs, but what made him truly terrifying was his anger. He roared and gnashed his teeth at Violet. Everyone in the village ran away to hide and escape the beast. But Violet did not run away. She did not hide; instead, she sang. She sang using words no one could later describe. She sang until the beast's roars could no longer be heard. She sang until he took in his last breath and fell to the ground with a loud thump next to Violet's feet. It was said after that day, the villagers were never again plagued with beasts. They said Violet slayed the beast with her song and her eyes, gifted by the gods.

There have only been a few rare stories told in history when one has come across a person with purple eyes. In those stories, the persons with purple eyes are extraordinary beings. They have great powers, although the extent of those powers is still relatively unknown. Many have said that those with purple eyes are descendants of the Egyptian gods. The first mention of such beings dates as far back as 2600 BC. Despite no real evidence of their existence, manticores are urged to stay away.

I shut the book and my eyes.

Could this be Michaela? Could she have extraordinary powers?

Despite my many years, I had never heard of such a story. Was this only manticore folklore, a story told to scare manticore children?

I leaned back against my chair and kept my eyes closed. I tried to conjure up her eyes. A vision of Michaela easily appeared in my mind. Her eyes were definitely purple—there was no mistaking them for any other color. But what did this mean for us? If she was not human, could we be together? Should she have nothing to fear from me? Was it me who should be fearful of her?

I opened my eyes and the book again. I flipped through a few more pages, but that was all that was said about purple eyes. The story suggested her song had killed the beast. If we manticores were the beasts, could she affect our hearts? Is that what James and I had felt back in his apartment? My research brought more questions and nothing that led me to believe we could be together.

I needed to find out more, talk to others who may have heard of this folklore. My father had two sisters, Elenora and Olympia, and a brother named Theodore. I would speak to Uncle Theodore. He'd travelled the world extensively; he might know more about the stories from Egypt. He'd be at the trial tomorrow. I planned to seek him out then.

Eight

Hunter

I arrived at the trial later than I'd intended. The courtroom was full and a few manticores stood in the back. It seemed every manticore in New York had shown up for this trial. I was not surprised since Jenkins had broken both rules of the Manticore Kingdom and there were only two: keep our existence a secret and never willfully harm a human. If a manticore broke one of these rules, he faced the king, who would determine his fate. It had been many years since one of us had broken our rules.

For centuries we'd lived on the fringe of society, afraid of how our predator instincts would react to humans. Many wanted to be a part of this civilization: their arts, their sports, their education system, their workforce. Slowly, a few stepped away from the shadows. My father and grandfather were among the first to do so.

The integration was not a success in the beginning. A few manticores fell in love with humans and discovered the heartbreaking ramifications of their union.

Others flaunted their powers and used fear to gain control. Any show of great strength, speed or impulsive anger was outlawed since it raised too many questions. Humans looked too closely at these particular attributes, which put manticores at risk of discovery.

My father found that with strict training and even stricter rules it was possible to live, work and play among humans. It was an enormous gain for the Manticore Kingdom, and my father became a hero: he brought us out of the shadows to live in the light.

Like all just rulers, the king created laws to maintain order. It was easy to abide by them, since manticores wanted to live and interact with the rest of the world's inhabitants. Rarely did one break the rules and jeopardize one's freedom and the kingdom's. But, just like we saw with Jenkins, it did happen. Now justice must be served.

Despite the standing room only, I maneuvered myself toward the front of the courtroom, where a seat was reserved for me next to my father. On my way there, I avoided speaking to anyone until I saw Thomas.

"Hey, Hunter," Thomas said.

"Everything under control?" I asked.

"Yes, all good. I spoke to Tony and the woman made it home that evening. So far, she has not mentioned the incident to anyone but her mom. We will keep surveillance a little longer, though, just in case."

"Thank you, Thomas," I said and stepped forward toward my seat.

"No problem. How's Laura?" he asked before I could walk past him.

"Laura? Oh, she's good. She's back in New York now. The premiere went well, I think. She may have even received an award at the film festival." Guilt hung on my conscience. I had forgotten about Laura. "She sent me a voice message about it."

"I knew she would kill it. I'll give her a call, just to congratulate her," said Thomas.

"You do that. I know she'd like to hear from you."

Thomas looked away. Now he was the one avoiding eye contact with me. I didn't know when he would decide to make his move for Laura or if he already had. Either way, I was staying out of it.

Sitting down, I scanned the room looking for Uncle Theodore.

I had hoped to speak with him before the trial began but I'd been busy this morning with a problem at work.

I didn't see Uncle Theodore in the seated section of the courtroom or among those standing. I searched for John, his son, but I couldn't find him either. Every seat in the room was taken, and if they arrived as late as I did, they probably wouldn't be able to find an unreserved seat. I resigned myself to looking for them afterward.

I'd been sitting only a few minutes when Lord Chancellor Lee entered the courtroom and asked us all to rise.

The doors opened again and my father glided in wearing his ceremonial robe and crown. He looked like a king and not the researcher I'd seen at the library last night. He wore his title with pride, his shoulders broad underneath the robe. He did not smile, and he walked with a straightness in his spine I had not seen in years. The hairs on the back of my neck rose.

"Everyone, please be seated," my father said.

"I am pleased to see so many of you here today, since the perpetrator's actions affect us all."

A murmur of agreement went through the crowd.

I looked at the predator locked in an iron cage. His hands were tied behind him. Confined like an animal. He didn't smile. He looked at the ground, shuffling his feet.

"Henry Jenkins stands before me accused of assaulting three humans. He bit, clawed and exposed his predator instincts, thereby threatening our secret and breaking the rules of the Manticore Kingdom," my father began.

He stopped momentarily to look at me and then continued. "I have made a decision and do not take this ruling lightly. I've spent hours researching past judgements, reading psychiatric evaluations of Jenkins, and listening to elders' opinions on the matter. I take my role as your king seriously. My motivations have always been to do what is right for manticores and what will preserve a sustainable future for generations of manticores to come."

I felt proud of my father.

"I researched instances where manticores were executed for simply stealing from another manticore. As those old enough will recall when we lived in the shadows, supplies and resources were low so thievery could not be taken lightly for our survival."

I nodded solemnly, thinking myself fortunate that I hadn't lived through those years.

"Today, this manticore stands before us not as a thief but as a rogue who assaulted three people."

"That's why we should execute him," a woman among those standing in the crowd shouted from the back. Whispers and nods of agreement waved through the room.

"Everyone, quiet," said Lord Chancellor Lee. And the room fell silent.

"I understand everyone's desire for swift justice," my father said. "I considered it, as well. His actions are not to be taken lightly. He will be punished."

He paused to look at Jenkins.

"I considered the punishment the accused would receive in the human world. There is a growing movement of rehabilitation in their justice system. The death penalty is abolished in many places around the world. Civilizations have moved away from meting out brutal sentences to criminals—like cutting off a hand or a head—but incarcerate them instead. Reformation and the perpetrator's ability to reform is part of this new world order, and I believe that we, too, should move forward in this direction. If we are to live amongst humans, we should try to understand their ways."

A woman gasped and brought a hand toward her mouth. I understood her shock but dared not interrupt my father.

"I have spoken to this manticore and believe he is capable of rehabilitation. He will never be allowed to leave this underground kingdom and for the next one hundred years will be assigned to his cage. But he will not be executed today."

At this declaration, I glanced at the predator. He was probing the crowd. He found someone and gave them a sly smile. A grin that showed neither relief nor even disbelief, but a cunning smile that somehow suggested he was the puppet master and we were his puppets.

I scanned the room again, stretched my neck hoping to catch a glimpse of someone returning that smile. But I couldn't pinpoint anyone. I glared back at the predator. He was looking down again, but a hint of that smile lingered on his face.

And then mayhem exploded in the room.

There were shouts from the back and those who were seated now stood and shouted back. Someone tried to rush toward the front, but a security guard stopped him. Another guard took the iron cage, which I realized was on wheels, and rolled it out of the room.

I worried someone would rush to hurt my father, feared that anarchy would erupt. I reached him in two strides.

"Father, we need to leave now."

"I will not run away with my tail between my legs. I am still the ruler here."

"Yes but..."

"Manticores of the Kingdom, stand down!" he shouted, and the boom of his voice froze my feet in place. He must've had the same effect on everyone else since no one moved or said another word. The room was silent again.

"Not all of you will agree with this judgement, but I expect you all to accept it. We are moving in a new direction and while that may be confusing and frightening at first, as your ruler, you will obey me. I promise you, I will be the rock and the foundation this new kingdom will be built on."

He pounded his fist on his chair when he said this. He glared at those who'd caused havoc in the room. They lowered their heads. When he was satisfied with his subjects' obedience, he turned and left the room.

Everyone started talking at once, but I did not stick around to hear what they said. Instead, I followed my father out of the room.

He was not in the hallway. But I knew where to find him. As a child, whenever I needed my father, I found him in his study. I walked the short distance to the room and opened the door.

He sat behind the large oak desk. His arms crossed over his chest, he stared at a painting on the wall. I didn't have to turn to see which one it was. I knew it was the painting of my mother. My father had had it commissioned shortly after they were married.

"She would have agreed with me today. She wanted us to evolve and be more civilized." His voice rang strong and sure.

"She probably would have, but that doesn't change what's happening out there. Father, are you sure you've done the right thing?" I asked, less confident of his decision than him.

"Evolution is not random, my son. We must continue to adapt to the changes around us. We must make changes too, even if they are uncomfortable, in order to evolve."

"Yes," I said and considered his words. "Or the changes may be a catalyst for revolution."

He was silent for a moment while he contemplated this.

"Does change bring on evolution or revolution?" He asked aloud and rubbed his chin. "I believe we shall see soon enough which one will come to pass."

***

After the chaos in the courtroom, Thomas said the manticores settled down quickly, most likely due to the king's direct order. The security team took care of anyone still shoving or shouting, and there weren't many of them left. The courtroom sat empty now, and only a few stragglers chatted in the hallways.

I could not ignore what had happened. I needed to find out what most of the kingdom thought of the decision. If there was any talk of discord, I needed to smooth it over right away.

Tony, Thomas and I stood in one of the anterooms next to the courtrooms. "Gentleman, have you heard anything further?" I asked them.

"No. The shouting stopped, and it appears everything is fine now," said Thomas.

"This decision must be accepted by everyone," I explained to them. "We need to assemble an advertising campaign emphasizing the new world justice." I turned toward Thomas. "Speak to Laura. She is certain to have ideas on how to get our message across."

"I'll go immediately," Thomas answered.

"Tell her this is not us showing weakness but the continuation of the path of integration for manticores. The path toward complete assimilation. Perhaps one day, we won't need to hide who we are. If we can control our instincts, even those for retribution, humans will have no reason to fear us. This is a good thing, the right thing, and we need to convey it as such."

"You're right, Hunter," said Thomas. "You know, you will be an incredible leader one day."

"Thanks, Thomas. I just don't want it to be today."

Today, I had a date. It would be my last day with Michaela.

I'd thought about it all last night and this morning. Even if she did have purple eyes and because of them, extraordinary abilities, it didn't mean she could be with a manticore. It didn't mean we could be together or that I could risk anything happening to her. No, this changed nothing. Tonight would be my last night with her. I would give myself this one final night but then it needed to end here in New York.

Nine

Michaela

Dev, this trip has turned out better than I could have imagined!" I said, balancing the phone against my cheek while I finished packing my suitcase. I had forgotten my earphones again.

My flight left at 8:00 a.m. the next morning. I didn't want to lose any sleep having to pack, so I'd decided to do it the night before.

It was 5:30 p.m. and I had thirty minutes before Hunter picked me up. I had already showered and done my hair and makeup. I had nothing to do except putter around until six. Talking to Dev saved me from second-guessing my clothes, my hair, my sanity. If I had extra time on my hands, I would probably overthink our date tonight. I would make myself nervous and cancel.

"The food at Savor was better than my morning cup of coffee," I told Dev as I paced around the room.

"Oh, that noodle dish you posted looked yummy enough to eat through my phone," he said, and we both laughed.

"Tricia is still upset over Vanessa's Instagram story. You know, the one where she alludes to her interview with James Norton," said Dev. "She still doesn't believe you were the one to set that up."

"Well, I didn't exactly set it up. Leo did. But I'll take credit if I must," I joked, placing my hand to my forehead.

"Which one is Leo again?" Dev asked.

"He's Hunter's cousin."

"That's right. I'm having a hard time keeping track of all the fine men you're working with now."

"Ha! Oh, I always knew New York would be my jam." I sighed into the phone.

"You're still coming home, aren't you? One of those New Yorkers hasn't swept you off your feet?"

"No, of course not. But I have a good feeling about Hunter. He makes me nervous, happy, and excited all at the same time. That's good, right?"

"Yes, it's very good. Are you willing to do the long-distance thing if the chemistry continues tonight?"

"I think so. It's not so bad. I had a long-distance relationship with Josh, remember."

Josh Rogan was my college sweetheart. Dev, Josh and I had all been friends in college. We'd met in Psych 101. But then Josh had transferred to a different university out of town.

"You call that long-distance? He went to Western University—that was only a two-hour drive away from us," he reminded me needlessly. I'd done the drive many times.

"It was two and *a half* hours, and you know he hardly came up on the weekends. He was busy studying," I said and busied myself with a scarf.

"Yep, studying all the new freshmen arriving on campus," Dev replied.

I scrunched up my nose because he was right. Josh was a terrible cheat. I was once on a video call with him and he didn't realize some girl's bra was hanging from his bathroom doorknob. Judging from the size of that bra, they could not have been real.

"Well, Hunter and I aren't college kids. We are two mature adults. If we like each other, I don't see why a small thing such as distance should keep us apart," I said, feeling more comfortable with the idea after having said it aloud.

"Well, I love your optimism. Me, I'm a realist. I want a guy who has a good job, pays his own bills, and makes me dinner. So long distance is out for me. You should consider the same—I've tasted your cooking."

I laughed out loud at this. I'd made a butternut squash soup for Dev once. The recipe called for a cup of apple cider, but for some reason my brain read apple cider vinegar. It was definitely not a good substitute.

"I'll think about it, Dev, but no promises. Love is unpredictable!" I said as I did a little pirouette.

"I better let you go. It's almost six," said Dev.

I double-checked the time on my phone.

"Oh, you're right. Talk to you tomorrow. I land at ten o'clock—maybe we can meet up for lunch? How's sushi?"

"Sounds good."

I ended the call and looked for my wedge sandals. I couldn't decide if I should be comfy or sexy and these were the perfect compromise.

Someone knocked on my suite door. It was exactly six o'clock—right on time. I loved that.

I opened the door and Hunter stood in the hallway with his hands in his pockets, looking relaxed and as yummy as the noodles at Savor. He wore a dark grey pair of trousers and a crisp white shirt. He had a bit of a five o'clock shadow on his face that I hadn't noticed the other day. He must have not shaved this morning.

I imagined the stubble would feel rough against my fingertips. I was tempted to reach and find out but knew it would be weird, so I flexed my fingers at my side to keep them busy.

"Michaela," he said with a devilish grin. He looked happy to see me. He also looked relieved, as if he wasn't sure if I would answer the door.

"Hunter, you look really...great," I said.

"Thank you, so do you." His eyes roamed over my outfit.

I'd decided on a navy blue wrap dress I'd picked up at a trunk sale last year. It was one of my favorites.

"Are you ready to go?" he asked.

"I am. Where are we going anyway?" I said as I grabbed my purse hanging near the door.

"I promised you some sightseeing and I'm going to deliver on that promise."

A big smile spread across my face. "Well then, let's go." A man who was prompt and made good on his promises. Yes, he was off to a very good start.

His cologne reminded me of the woods and I smiled, imagining him in a forest in a suit and tie. He walked with me down the hallway toward the elevator. When the doors opened, I heard Hunter say, "After you."

He followed me inside and the doors closed.

It was one of those mirrored elevators and it was just the two of us inside. I felt his stare on me and looked up. At first, I avoided looking directly at him but stared at his reflection in the mirror instead. If I saw a man stare like that at any other woman, I would have blushed from my neck down to my toes, but since the stare was directed at me, I was a little nervous. He looked so intense, like he was memorizing every detail on my face.

I turned to look at him and his amber eyes bore into mine. Strangely, his eyes were a little different right now. They reminded me of my cat, Mr. Whiskers. Whenever he stared outside into the sunshine, his pupils constricted to a nearly vertical line. Hunter's weren't as distinct as a cat's but they did look similar. What strange eyes.

"Your eyes... They're different," I said to calm my nerves.

He blinked rapidly and stared straight ahead.

"What do you mean?" he asked but didn't look at me.

"I don't know, but they remind me of a cat I once had, Mr. Whiskers."

He coughed and laughed into his fist at the same time.

"Well, did Mr. Whiskers ever tell you that you are the most beautiful woman he's ever seen?" he said as he turned toward me again.

"No, but he did like to lick my fingers and bite my wrist when he was playful."

I wouldn't mind if you did that either.

He gave me this strange look, like he was thinking the same thing, and I couldn't help but laugh.

What was it about elevators?

The doors finally opened and we walked to the front of the hotel. Hunter greeted the doorman who stood stoically next to a shiny black sports car waiting out front. I recognized it to be a Scorpion, because I'd done a lot of research before pitching this particular car manufacturer once.

"I'm a fan of the M94 model," I heard myself say. I shook my head. I didn't know why I'd said that. It sounded as though I was putting down his car.

"Are you, now? Looks like I will have to work on changing your mind."

My last boyfriend would have explained why this one was superior, or perhaps that I didn't understand cars. But not Hunter. No, he would work for my approval. He got better and better.

I slid my legs onto the soft leather seat and inhaled the woodsy smell that permeated the interior and was uniquely Hunter.

"So, Hunter," I said. I loved saying his name out loud. "Were you born and raised a New Yorker?"

"No. I've lived in several places but came to New York about...ah...fifteen years ago."

"Mmm...and how old are you exactly?"

"A man never reveals his age."

"I thought that was a woman?"

"I believe in equal rights and equal nondisclosure of age."

"Okay, fair enough, even though I think it's weird you don't want to tell me your age. How about I guess?"

When he didn't respond, I went on. I should have been a reporter.

"From what you've told me about your job and your role in it, you must have been working there for some time. You're not married and don't have any kids, but that really doesn't mean anything...mmm...okay, stab in the dark here...are you twenty-eight?"

"No."

"Thirty-five, then"

"No."

"Forty?"

He didn't respond.

"You're really not going to tell me?" I asked.

"I will never lie to you, Michaela," he said solemnly, too serious for this line of questioning.

"But omission of the truth is the same as lying, isn't it?" I said with a smirk.

"Fine. I'm 105."

I laughed, because how absurd was that. I decided to let the age thing go. It seemed to be a touchy subject for him.

"Okay, fine, I'll leave it alone...for now. In case you're wondering, I'm twenty-six."

"I know."

"You do? How do you know that?"

"I researched you a little. Your bio is on Sway PR's website and you've published a few blogs on your own website," he said with a smile. "It's a great source of information, especially if I want to know your pet peeves and which is your favorite book this month."

"You Googled me?"

His honesty was refreshing, as I had done the same with him.

"You graduated from the University of Toronto with honors, then received a master's in communication. Your first job out of college was with a boutique PR firm but that only lasted six months because Sway PR scooped you up. You've been there ever since."

"Huh," I said, a bit impressed. That wasn't all in my bio so he must have researched a bit more than one search hit.

"Also, in your blog you write about how much you love to paint, play the violin and read romance novels. I love Lisa Kleypas too, by the way."

"Oh my God! You read romance novels!" I shouted back.

He laughed. "My sister Laura once told me it was the best way to understand women, so I dutifully did my research."

"Admit that you love them and it's not just research," I teased.

His laugh was beautiful; I felt giddy just listening to it.

"Fine, but you're not allowed to tell anyone," he said and pointed a finger at me.

"I can't promise you that. I think it's one of your most endearing qualities."

The look he gave me was one of pure joy, and I couldn't help but be happy around him.

He turned left into a driveway leading to a condo building. It was modern with plenty of windows. Instead of concrete, white smooth stone covered the front entrance, which made the black wooden doors pop.

"We're here," he said as he pulled up to the front doors. "Come on."

He sounded as excited as I felt.

A doorman opened my car door. I stepped out and tried to peer up to the top of the building, but it was so darn high that the top was lost in the night sky.

He led me through the grand foyer. The floors were white porcelain tiles bordered with black marble. Black iron railings with gold trim framed a staircase that led to an open mezzanine. Instead of taking the carpeted staircase, Hunter guided me with a light hand on my lower back toward the shiny elevators.

"I promise to behave this time," he said with a smirk as the doors opened and we got in.

Too bad.

He placed an access card against a pad on the elevator menu and then pressed the "R" button at the top.

It took a few minutes for the elevator to carry us up. My stomach felt a little queasy as the elevator moved quickly toward its destination.

Please don't throw up on his beautiful leather shoes.

The elevator finally stopped. When the doors opened, they unveiled the night sky.

We're on the rooftop!

I walked out slowly, wanting to take everything in at once. There were boxwood hedges in planter boxes all around the perimeter. Small patio lights twinkled along the hedges, giving the space a cozy glow. A carpet that reminded me of faux grass was laid out in the center with at least a dozen pillows scattered around it. The brightly colored pillows reminded me of a Persian restaurant I'd gone to once. I remembered the silk being soft and inviting.

"If the carpet and pillows are not comfortable, I can ask Robbie to bring up the divan," said Hunter, noticing where my gaze landed.

"No, no," I started to explain. "Wait, you did all this?"

"Yes. I wanted to have a private picnic under the stars, and this was the perfect place."

"Picnic..." And then I spied the baskets sitting next to the carpet. Hunter walked over and opened them.

"Please, sit down. Do you prefer white or red wine?" he said while pulling items out of the baskets.

"White, please," I responded and stretched my neck to sneak a peek at what was inside.

He opened a bottle that sat chilling in an ice bucket next to the baskets.

"These are some of my favorite dishes from Amelie's."

He passed me a platter of cheeses, cured meats, olives and fruit. He then poured me a glass of wine and one for himself.

"To you," he said, raising his glass. "And to making the most of tonight."

I liked the sound of that. We clinked glasses and I took a sip. It was delicious.

He handed me a plate and I had no shame in filling it. It all looked so good.

"So, tell me about yourself," I said while I started on the cheese platter.

"There isn't much to tell," said Hunter, looking a little uncomfortable. Maybe it was the carpet; maybe not.

"Do you have any siblings?" I asked.

"Yes, a sister. Her name is Laura," he said with a smile. This one reached his eyes. "Actually, she was in Toronto recently. She premiered her documentary at the film festival there." Then after a slight pause, he added, "I attended the after-party with her."

"Oh, which one?" I said, as I tried to spear a raspberry.

"The Hugo Boss one." He looked away from my gaze.

"What?" I couldn't believe the coincidence. "I was there too. I could have run into you."

"Yes, I know," he said, and then a little bit softer added, "I saw you."

"You what?" I asked, confused. "You did?"

"Yes. You were dancing and then some guy came up from behind and started pawing at you," he said. This time he speared the raspberry with more force than I thought necessary.

"Huh, I remember that. He was a terrible dancer, but it was fun," I said, recalling that night. And then a glimmer of a flashback: me dancing, laughing, looking up around me. I see a tall man on the balcony staring out onto the dance floor. He looks handsome but I don't get a chance to really notice him because some guy grabs me from behind and we start to dance.

"That was you? The one on the balcony?" I asked, but I was certain it had to have been Hunter.

"Yes," he responded in a low voice.

"Wow, we were both in two separate cities together twice in one week. That's quite a coincidence."

"Or fate," he said, looking up at the stars.

I smiled because I liked the sound of that better. But his face was serious, no smile lingered there.

"Okay, so there's Laura. Any brothers?" I asked, trying to get his good humor back.

"No, no brothers. I do have cousins, though. You've met Leo, and I have another one named John," he said. "My mother passed away some years ago, but my father is very much alive."

"Tell me about him." I wanted to know everything about this man.

"He is quite a force." He smiled, again, and my heart did a little dance in my chest. "He's strong and fierce but he doesn't allow those traits to lead him. Instead, he lets his unwavering sense of compassion and willingness to always see the best in others pave his decisions. He makes you believe you can become more than you thought you could be." I heard pride in his words as he described his father.

"He sounds like quite a man," I said, looking up at Hunter.

"He is that and more—" and then he corrected himself "—at least to me."

"I would love to meet him one day," I said and then cringed because I realized how forward that sounded. I didn't feel any better when Hunter ignored it and changed the subject.

"What about you? Do you have any siblings?" he asked. While I hated talking about my family life, I welcomed the change in subject.

"No, I'm an only child. My mother had me later in life and she said I was all she needed. Even though I'm sure she said that just to make me feel special." My mouth turned up in a smile at the memory of my mom holding me in her arms. She would soothe me until I fell asleep. "She always knew what to say. Whether there was a bully at school or my heart broke because a boy I liked didn't like me back. She would say, 'Michaela, you cannot let anyone else determine your worth, only you can decide that. And you are an incredibly special girl. You must recognize your own gifts before you can make anyone else appreciate them. Otherwise, it won't mean much to you to be validated by others.'"

"Sounds like she was a smart woman and a great mother," said Hunter, moving closer to me on the carpet. I welcomed his embrace when he put his arm around my shoulder. I leaned back against him. I stared up at the stars, feeling like my mother could be one of those bright lights up there, always looking down on me.

"When my parents died, my aunt came to live with me," I continued, feeling safe in his arms. "She is loving, caring and everything I could have asked for. But she could never replace what I lost."

This was why I hated talking about family. I inevitably thought about my parents and how their death had never really made sense to me. *I don't know if any child could comprehend losing a parent.*

Hunter noticed my melancholy. He stood up and pulled me up to my feet.

"I promised you some sights and I intend on showing them to you, but from the comfort of this rooftop," he explained.

I was a little confused but didn't say anything when he moved toward one of the hedges. He lifted the lid on a brown storage box and pulled out a telescope. Wow, he'd really thought of everything.

"I hope you don't mind. I thought I could share New York with you from up above."

"I love it," I said, genuinely excited by the prospect. I walked over to stand behind the telescope lens. "Oh, my goodness. I can't believe how much I can see from up here."

He moved the telescope a bit to the right. "Let's start with the lady first. The Statue of Liberty is right over here."

It looked small from up here. "I always imagined the Statue of Liberty so much bigger."

"It probably feels that way up close." He chuckled.

"Then we have the Empire State Building here, and the Chrysler Building there. People have strong opinions on which one they prefer," he explained, and I took in everything he showed me with pleasure. "That's the Brooklyn Bridge, and Central Park, of course."

"Wow, now that's bigger than I thought it would be." I laughed, amazed by the amount of green space in a busy metropolitan city.

"Yes, Central Park is much more than what you can see here, more than people can imagine." His voice sounded far away when he described the park.

"Perhaps I should take a carriage ride through it the next time I visit."

"You should. Perhaps I'll be the one to take you," he said but then shook his head. "Over here is the 9/11 Memorial."

I frowned at the loss of life that day. Hunter took a moment, as well.

"Wall Street is there," he said while moving the telescope up, "and up here are Broadway and Fifth Avenue."

"Yes, I've been to Fifth Avenue," I said with a grin.

He chuckled. "Did you buy something on Fifth that makes you smile like that?"

"I did not." I sighed. "But I did a ton of window shopping the other day," I added with a smirk.

He shook his head, smiled back, and continued. "This right here is one of my favorites. It's St. Patrick's Cathedral. It was built in 1879."

"Oh, are you Catholic?" I asked.

"No, I do not belong to any religious denomination. However, I do believe in God."

"I was raised Catholic and went to Catholic school. I haven't been to church in years, though," I said. "So, why is St. Patrick's one of your favorites, then?"

"I went in one time," he said and looked down at his hands. "My friend was murdered in front of me. I wanted to kill the other guy myself with my own bare hands, but I managed to walk away. I walked through the streets, barely seeing where I went. I hadn't even realized which building I had walked into until I found myself surrounded by pews."

Hunter took a breath. "I sat down, closed my eyes, and tried to regain control. I thought about what had made me so angry and what I was going to do about it, but that only made it worse. I began to pant. My chest heaved. I wanted to stand up and leave when a priest came and sat down beside me, blocking my exit."

Hunter looked away. "He didn't say a word, just sat there. I didn't want to hurt him, so I focused on getting my anger under control. I needed to still my racing blood. I sat and I listened to my breaths until they were slower, until I calmed down."

He looked at me now. "I don't know how long I sat there but it was dark by the time I left. Now, when I feel my temper rising, I try to take deep breaths to calm down. I don't ever want to let myself get that angry again."

"But why would that be one of your favorites?" I asked, confused that a place with such a bad memory would be one of his favorites and a little shocked that he'd nearly killed someone.

"Because," he said, looking out into the sky, "it set me in the right direction to change, to becoming a worthier being than some angry beast."

I didn't know how to respond to that. I couldn't imagine the person before me as the angry individual he'd just described.

"I can't picture you angry. You seem like you wouldn't let anything bother you," I told him, and I believed it. He seemed so cool and calm about everything, while I always felt like a champagne bottle ready to pop and spew out my opinion at the slightest provocation.

"Oh, plenty bothers me. I used to revel in my anger. I used it as fuel to fight against those that wronged me or my family. My anger made my blood race through my veins. It made my reflexes faster. But, to make good decisions, the right decisions, you need a cool head. If I didn't learn to control my anger, I wouldn't be any better than the ones who had wronged me. I, too, would just be acting on instinct."

"Not all instincts are bad," I said.

"Mine usually are."

"I'm feeling a particular instinct right now," I teased as I leaned toward his mouth and kissed him. I thought I was ready for the emotions that usually accompany a great kiss: the excitement, the fervor, the heat. What I wasn't prepared for was Hunter pushing me away.

"Michaela," he said my name and it sounded like a prayer on his lips. A guiding whisper in a dark room.

Encouraged, I leaned forward again, but he stopped me with his words.

"I, ah, I have one more surprise for you."

"I don't need any more surprises—this was all so great," I said and moved a little closer.

"Well, um, I think you're going to like this one," he said. He stood up and made an effort to straighten the wrinkles out of his clothes, even though they looked perfectly pressed to me.

"Okay, what's the surprise?" I asked, skeptically.

"Let me show you. Just give me one minute to make sure it's ready." He walked over to the other end of the rooftop, where he'd left his jacket, and then pulled out his phone. I didn't hear what he said but his voice sounded rushed and low. He ended the call and came back to me.

"All right, we're ready to go. Trust me, you're going to love this."

His smile had me smiling back and forgetting about kissing him—for a little while.

"Okay, I have to admit I do love surprises. Where are we going now?"

"We're going to Fifth Avenue, to do more than window shop."

Ten

Hunter

I had to think fast. When Michaela kissed me, I felt the blood rush to my lips. It felt as though every cell in my body wanted to be in contact with her. My heart raced and my instincts fought to take control and lay her down on those pillows and explore every inch of her. But I wasn't sure if I could stop there. I wasn't sure if I could stop. Period. That's why I had to think fast and think of something that would distract us both. I remembered what she'd said about Fifth Avenue, and I had an idea. I walked to the other end of the rooftop, so she couldn't hear me call my friend Cynthia.

Cynthia owned a designer shop on Fifth Avenue, and I knew her style would be perfect on Michaela. So, I asked Cynthia if she would allow me a private shopping experience at her store. She was a little surprised when I said it would be tonight, but she agreed and gave me the code to her security system. I was humbled by her trust in me and promised to make it up to her.

I drove to the shop called Fierce, a little slower than I normally would, wanting to calm my instincts and my lust. I took deep breaths the entire car ride there, but I still didn't feel completely in control of myself.

I parked the car and asked her to wait. I jogged up to the front door and punched in the alarm code Cynthia had given me. The green light flashed, and I checked the door. It opened without a hitch. I looked back at the car and Michaela's face glowed with excitement.

This might be the best idea I've ever had.

I walked back to the car and opened Michaela's door.

"Ready?" I asked as I held out my hand to help her out of the car. Her delicate fingers wrapped around my palm, and I couldn't resist. I gently brushed the pad of my ring finger along the inside of her hand. She snapped her head up to look at me, but I stared straight ahead and escorted her inside the store.

"Wow, these are beautiful," she said as she surveyed the shop and examined the clothes pinned on the mannequins.

"This is my friend Cynthia's place. She's quite talented."

"She's amazing. Although I'm not surprised since you know James Norton. You must know other talented designers too."

"Yes, I have a few friends in the creative field."

"I'm sure you do."

"Pick out anything you like. You can try them on in the fitting room in the back."

She turned over one of the tags on a gold-sequined dress.

"Oh, wow. Hunter, I really appreciate you bringing me here, but I can't afford these clothes."

"Don't look at the prices. It's on me."

"I couldn't possibly ask you to pay for me."

"You're not asking. I'm offering."

She stared at me and a small smile played on her lips. Her finger tapped the tag. "Okay, maybe just one or two pieces," she said.

Her smile faded and her eyebrows narrowed. She took to the clothing aisles like a captain on a mission. It was impressive.

She didn't look up from the rows for some time. She would make quite the predator if she were a manticore.

I didn't let the serious face fool me; she was having a great time. Her lips curved up and her eyes sparkled right before she picked out an item. She held it up and, if it passed her initial inspection, she flung it across her other arm and continued to search. There was something oddly endearing about watching her shop. It reminded me of something a normal couple would do. Something I could watch her do over and over again.

It was about thirty minutes later, after I had relieved her of her pile twice already, when she finally said, "I'm ready to try these on."

I led her to the back of the shop and showed her to the fitting rooms. There was a plush pink carpet in the center of the room and a gold framed mirror at the end. On one side there were three curtained-off rooms, and white couches had been placed just in front of them. I made myself comfortable on one of the couches.

I checked my phone for messages, but there wasn't anything urgent. I was relieved nothing had come up since today's courtroom decision, but I wasn't naïve enough to think everyone was fine with it. We would get a campaign going, and everyone would get on board. I told myself this while a tiny voice of dissent wormed through my mind.

I looked up from my phone when movement from the other side of the room grabbed my attention. Michaela hadn't closed the curtain completely, and I caught a glimpse of her delicate arm on the other side. Then her leg came into view; she wore black panties and a matching lace bra. Her skin was smooth and looked as soft as velvet. Her curves spilled out of the fabric a bit, not wanting to be constrained.

This was the worst idea I've ever had.

A suffocating heat crept along my neck and my muscles strained to reach out to her. My body urged me to go to her, but my mind screamed that I had no right. If I cared about her, I'd stay away from her. I chanted this thought in my head. I closed my eyes and didn't open them until I was in control. Until I knew I could walk away from her and not rip that curtain down.

I slowly stood up, held my breath, and walked out of the fitting rooms. The cool air on the other side of the shop made it easier to breathe. I took a deep breath in and let it out slowly. I waited there, until she emerged from the changeroom.

"Hunter? Where did you go?" she called.

"I'm out here."

"Oh, can you tell me what you think of this one?"

I warned myself to be strong—I could do this. She was only human. She didn't have any special power over me.

I was a strong, powerful, deadly manticore. I could handle an outfit change.

I walked back to the fitting room where Michaela wore the gold-sequined dress. I never thought I would covet sequins as much as I did at that moment.

"You're gorgeous," I said. I couldn't think of anything more original. My brain had melted.

"I tried on some other things in the room that I'm not going to get but I wasn't sure about this one. Do you think the sequins are too much? Do they scream 'look at me'?"

"No. As bright as the sequins are, you outshine them."

She looked at me, her head slanted to the side, and stared. "I'm trying to figure out if you're serious right now," she said.

"I've never been more serious in all my life."

"All right, I think I'll get it," she said, smoothing the dress down her hips in front of the mirror. "Hope I have someplace to wear it, though."

I exhaled, relieved I didn't have to convince her any further. She was going to get that dress if I had to smuggle it into her suitcase myself. No one else could ever do it justice. It was made for her.

"I'm just going to take this off and then I'm done. I'm going to take the dress and the white blouse, if that's okay."

"That's perfect," I said and turned away.

I walked toward the exit of the store to stop myself from following her into the fitting room and helping her take the dress off.

"I'll just be outside for a second. I need to make a phone call."

While that was only an excuse to get away from her siren call and her tempting scent, I decided to call Thomas while I was out there.

"Hey, Thomas, how are things?"

"Everything seems okay. The kingdom and hallways are quiet. Your father just left. He said he was going home for the rest of the night. Jenkins is locked up and there hasn't been any protest since his trial. Where are you?"

I briefly explained to Thomas where I was and whom I was with.

"You're playing with fire, Hunter. And you know what they say about those who play with fire."

Yes, and I was already burning.

"She leaves tomorrow. It will all be over then," I said.

"Well, for your sake as much as hers, I hope you're right."

Michaela opened the shop door at that moment and our eyes connected.

"I have to be right. There's no other way." And I ended the call.

"Who was that?" she asked.

"My friend Thomas."

"Is he the one who was at Savor with you?"

"Yes, Thomas and John were with me. Thomas was the one to my right."

She looked down and chewed on her thumbnail before she said, "Oh okay, he's the happier one."

"Happier?" I asked.

"Yes, the other guy looked like he was scowling at you, as if you'd said something to upset him."

"That's just John. He's always angry about something." I leaned forward to open her car door and this time she waited for me to do so. I liked that she already knew this was something I would always do for her.

"So, where are we going next?" she asked with a look of expectation I hated to deny.

"Well, I've got an early meeting tomorrow, so I think I'm going to have to take you back to your hotel."

"Oh," she said and got into the car. I walked back to the shop to set the alarm and took a minute to e-transfer Cynthia more than enough funds to cover Michaela's dress and blouse.

I returned to my car and started the engine. I drove down the streets of New York in silence. I didn't know what to say. "It's not you, it's me" was not going to work. Different explanations rioted in my mind. She, however, was the first one to speak.

"I don't want to play coy or play any games with you," she said. "I like you and I know we live in different cities, but I'd like to still talk to you and see where this can go."

It can't go anywhere. Nothing can grow from a relationship between the two of us. It will not make you happy and it will only torture me.

My thoughts hardened my resolve. "You're a great girl, Michaela, but..."

"Stop. Don't say it's you and not me."

"I know it sounds cliché, but there are things you don't know about me that would probably scare you if you did."

When I stopped at the traffic light, I took the opportunity to look her in the eye for the next part. She deserved to know what I told her was the truth and not some line. Her eyes lost their glowing excitement at the serious look on my face. The goosebumps on her arms told me a shiver ran through her at the same time she straightened her shoulders.

"I think you feel it, the dark side of me," I whispered and reached for her hand.

She didn't deny it. She remained silent until I parked in one of the spots in front of her hotel entrance. She turned to me then. "I do feel a darkness inside you, but it's not evil. It's just something you want to hide from the world, a secret you want hidden from others."

Stunned by her perception, I didn't know what to say to it. Fortunately, or maybe unfortunately, she continued.

"I'm not afraid of it, Hunter, whatever it is inside you. Because I can handle it. I lost my parents when I was young. I lived with an aunt who believed she could speak to dead people. I've had to deal with darkness in my life. I'm not afraid of it." She said this last part with such fierceness in her eyes that I almost told her. "Let me in. I want to help you," she said softly.

I shook my head because she had no idea.

"You can't save me, Michaela. I cannot be saved. Someone like you can never be with someone like me. Ever. That doesn't mean I don't want you. That doesn't mean when I look at you, I don't want to claim you with everything inside of me. That doesn't mean I don't go into a jealous frenzy when someone looks at you with lust in his eyes. None of that changes the fact that we can't be together."

She was a little taken aback by my declaration. I might have come on a little strong. But, dammit, she needed to understand it really was me—or what I am—that kept us apart. Not her, not this fierce, passionate woman.

"I don't understand. If you have those impulses and emotions, why don't you want to give this a try?"

How to make her understand...

"Because no matter how much a man wants to fly, he doesn't try it because he knows it will kill him. Because no matter how much a mermaid may want to walk on land with her sailor, she doesn't try it because she will not survive it. I wouldn't survive being with you and not ever being able to have you."

"I don't understand what that means. Why not?"

"There's a lot about the world you know, Michaela, and there's more you don't know. You may walk this earth and read its history, but these stories have been written for you and your kind."

"I may not have lived in this world as long as you have, Hunter—however old you are—but I'm not naïve. I don't want to save you. I just want to spend more time with you. But that's fine. If it's not what you want, I wish you would have just said that instead of talking in riddles and suggesting I'm naïve."

"Michaela, wait!" I said as she stepped out of the car. She walked toward the hotel entrance, but I stopped her before she could get inside. I had my hands on her shoulders when she gently took them off, one by one.

"It's fine, Hunter. I'm fine. Really. This big girl can take care of herself. Thank you for the sights and the shopping. And I wish you a nice life."

"Michaela, please."

But it was too late. She left.

I wanted to run after her but what was the point? What could I say to make her understand without breaking one of our rules? She couldn't understand. Maybe if she hated me it would make this easier on her, although it was killing me.

Frustration boiled inside my gut, churning with every question I raised. Why did she have to be human? Why did the essence of me kill her? Why couldn't there be a way for us to be together? Please God, did I not deserve love?

My emotions made me frantic, and I didn't trust myself to be alone.

I decided to see Thomas. I would drink all his whiskey and sleep until I finally forgot those fierce violet eyes.

Hunter

My phone buzzed but it was too far to reach. I didn't have the energy to get up. It buzzed again, and this time it sounded louder but only because the fog was slowly lifting from my brain. I couldn't recall how much whiskey I'd drunk, or even how I got into this bed, but I did remember shouting and then breaking furniture. And then I remembered nothing at all. Until this incessant buzzing.

The buzzing finally—thankfully—stopped, only to be replaced with Thomas's voice in the other room. I couldn't quite make out what he was saying. I normally could hear a whisper, but I wasn't trying to listen carefully. Instead, I tried to go back to sleep.

I knew I wouldn't be getting any sleep when Thomas burst through the door.

"Hunter, you have to get up."

"Go away."

"No, you have to get up."

"Thomas, I am warning you now, let me be."

"It's about the king!"

My brain was still foggy, but I did register those words and the panic in his voice. I slowly rose from the bed using my forearms. "What is wrong with my father?"

"A maid entered his room this morning and opened the window curtains, as usual. However, when the king did not stir, she moved closer to see if he was all right. She said he was deathly pale and didn't seem to be breathing. She panicked and screamed for the entire household to hear, 'The king is dead!'"

"Why didn't anyone call me?"

"They did. You didn't answer, so they called me next."

"Dear God, my father cannot be dead."

"The physician is there now, seeing if anything can be done."

"Let's go. He cannot be dead. He cannot."

Thomas insisted on driving, and I did not argue. Thoughts screamed in my head. He was healthy, how could this have happened? Visions of yesterday's courtroom chaos—manticores yelling and raging. Could someone have murdered my father? It could have been anyone. I hadn't paid attention to their faces, only listened to their voices. I scanned my memory to recall the voices. Did any of those voices sound familiar? I was nearly certain I heard the voice of Tommy Ross. He was a traditionalist and always against progress. I made a mental note to seek him out.

There were dozens of other voices in my head, but I couldn't name them all. I had a difficult time thinking of anything other than my father. He could not be dead!

Thomas pulled up into the mansion's long driveway and turned off the engine when we reached the front doors. I ran out of the car like some avenging angel. I took the stairs to my father's room two at a time and rushed through the open door.

The room was filled with people. Aunt Elenora and her son, Leo, were there. As were Uncle Theodore and his son, John. My father's youngest sibling, Olympia, sat in a chair in the far corner, her head in her hands. The scene did not bode well for him.

The physician stood next to my father's bed but stared at me. I turned my gaze to look down and gathered my courage to face my fears. My father lay still. His hands were as pale as the sheet underneath them. I faced the elderly doctor and asked him the question I feared most: "Is my father dead?"

"We believed so at first," he said. "He did not awaken when he was jostled, and he did not appear to be breathing. However, upon closer inspection, I have found a faint heartbeat and a very shallow breath. He still lives...for now."

"What do you mean, for now?"

"Well, I was leaning in for some time, listening for a heartbeat, when I also detected a strange smell nearby."

I edged closer to the bed. I couldn't stop myself from grabbing my father's hand and falling to my knees before his bed. I laid my head on his hand and that's when I smelled it too. Yes, a sweet but pungent scent.

"I smell it too. What is it?"

"It is chrysanthemum," said the physician.

Confused, I shook my head. "The flower?"

"Yes. It is poisonous to cats and can make manticores quite sick."

"You cannot tell me that a flower can bring down the King of Manticores. We've never been warned of this."

"Well, yes, but mainly because manticores for centuries have eaten the same substance as humans, and most humans do not eat chrysanthemums. It is not part of their diet. It's never been necessary to warn manticores not to eat them as many would not find the smell appetizing. However, it's not just chrysanthemums in this concoction. It is also laced with a poison I cannot identify but one that I do faintly detect. I believe the combination is slowly killing your father. He is lucky. Had he not sputtered most of the poison out, he would be dead right now."

Someone let out a gasp, but I did not turn to see who it was.

My father had been poisoned. Someone had tried to kill him, and he may still die.

"What can we do, Doctor? There must be something," I pleaded with him.

"I have taken a swab of your father's mouth. I will take it back to my team at the lab to analyze it. I hope we can find an antidote that will counteract the effects of the poison. I fear, however, that we do not have much time."

"What can I do?"

"Be patient," he said to me.

"I have to do something else. I must find the person who did this. I will kill him with my own hands," I said. My hands began to shake, and I felt myself losing control of my temper.

A whisper from the back of the room caught my attention and I turned around. Everyone looked among themselves to see who it was when Aunt Olympia stood up from her chair.

"We need to find the one with the violet eyes," she said softly.

I was stunned. She couldn't have said that. "What did you say?"

Louder this time, she said, "Find the one with the violet eyes."

"Why?" I asked in disbelief. She could not mean Michaela. What did my aunt know of her? Did she see her in my father's room last night? No, it couldn't be. She flew back to Toronto, miles away from here.

"I've always been the quiet one," continued Aunt Olympia. "As a child, I would sit in the back of a room and play with my dolls as the adults would discuss important matters without realizing I was there. I recall a time when our grandmother's sister was seriously ill, on the verge of death, and she demanded that they call the one with the violet eyes. I didn't know what it meant then, and I still do not know now. But she got better after that. I think this person can save Marsel. It may be our only chance. Violet eyes may be our only hope."

I snapped my head to look at Leo. I wanted to know if he was thinking what I was thinking. He had seen Michaela's eyes up close.

"Michaela," I said softly while staring at Leo.

"No, it's not her," said Leo adamantly. "You just want an excuse to see her again, but don't get her involved in this."

"I don't want to get her involved, but what if Aunt Olympia is right? What if she's our only hope?"

"She's not. What if you tell her about us, break our biggest rule, and she is nothing but a mortal human? What then, huh?" he shouted. "Then, you have put not just yourself in danger but the entire kingdom. It's too risky."

"I will not tell her who we are. I am just going to find out what she knows about her eyes." Leo shook his head. Frustrated that he would not support me, I shouted back, "Dammit Leo, we have to do something."

"We should be patient. We wait to see what the physician discovers. He will find the antidote. He will."

"I can't take the chance that he won't," I said, completely wrecked by the prospect.

"Go find this Michaela," Aunt Olympia urged. "Be careful how you approach her, but I believe she may be the answer to our prayers."

"Thank you, Aunt Olympia," I said, relieved that I had someone on my side. "I'm going to get on the next flight to Toronto and see what she knows."

I stormed out of the room before anyone had the chance to stop me with any further reproach. This was the reason Michaela had come into my life, I was sure of it. It was the reason I felt something more within her. It wasn't just about me; she might be the only one who could save the Manticore King.

With that resolved in my head, I raced down the stairs and to the car. Thomas still sat in the driver's seat.

"I'm going to Toronto to find Michaela," I said. He just nodded at this information. Thomas must have sensed there was no point in trying to talk me out of it.

"What can I do?" he asked.

"I need you to keep a surveillance on Tommy Ross. I heard him in the courtroom yesterday, blasting the decision. Keep an eye on him and make sure he had nothing to do with the attempt to assassinate the king. If it is him, he will get the traditional decision he wanted and he will be executed at once. I will personally behead the traitor myself."

Eleven

Michaela

The Canadian PR plan will be vastly different from the US approach," I said to a boardroom filled with general managers, VPs, and sales directors. "When you launched this new line of products in the US, there was a tremendous amount of backlash toward the visuals used to promote the brand. They were not reflective of the brand's target audience—in fact, they were the complete opposite. This is why there was so much bad press and negative social media around the launch."

I clicked the remote and it flipped to the next slide of our PR plan.

"Sway PR will put forth a plan that does not alienate any potential consumer, and especially does not alienate those who built this company," I continued. "We will ensure that the core demographic is not just included but is leading the conversation for the brand. There will be exclusive media presentations for this core group and their influencers. They'll be the first to test the new products. We understand you want to grow your customer base, but this must be done in a thoughtful, tactful, and strategic way. You cannot lose perspective."

This presentation was a risk. We knew going into this meeting we were going to present this client with a PR plan vastly different from what their US agency did. And no one wanted to be told what they did was wrong. But, based on our market research, the brand's voice was not faring well in media and social media in the US. We needed to ensure that would not happen when they launched here in Canada. To be blunt, their last agency had been tone deaf. They didn't understand why their message had received such negative publicity, and it was not easy to be the one to tell a client their last plan sucked.

Tricia and I had worked through lunches, dinners and nights on this strategy and presentation. We discussed how we could do better and came up with some innovative ideas. Suzanne said she would back us up, and now the only obstacle was getting the client on board.

Tricia took over the next few slides and did a fantastic job of making the room laugh. There were a couple of stone-cold faces, but I had seen it before with those in authority. They wanted to hide their thoughts, or even hide the fact that they were having fun.

"So, you're saying you want us to change all our photography?" asked a white-haired gentleman seated at the front. He was one of the sales managers, I thought. I had a feeling the previous photo session was his idea.

"Yes. We feel that the original imagery did not take the core demographic into consideration and the previous campaign photos made them turn away from the brand. Here's what we're thinking." I pulled up a slide we had prepared earlier, in the event this question came up. We wanted to be prepared for anything.

The slide depicted men, women, families, friends—all in different settings—enjoying the products. It was fresh, fun, and most importantly inclusive.

"I don't see why we would need to reshoot everything," mumbled the man in the front seat.

"Thank you, Tricia and Michaela, for presenting your ideas to us," said Tasha. She was one of the VPs. "We will discuss your strategy among ourselves and get back to you later in the week with our decision. Thank you for coming in."

"Thank you for having us. It was great to meet you all." And with that, Tricia and I grabbed our laptops and left the boardroom.

We kept silent until we were safely inside the elevators. I waited for the chrome doors to close and then finally exhaled. "Whoa, that was crazy," I said. "I was nervous and excited the entire time. A few kept their poker faces throughout the entire presentation. I'm not sure if we'll get it. How do you think we did?"

"We killed it," Tricia said unconcerned.

"How are you so sure?" I asked.

"I had a psychic reading last night and he said I would nail a big presentation. And I did. I'm not worried—you shouldn't be either."

"I wish I had your confidence," I said. She looked at me and shrugged, like it wasn't likely that I would ever have it.

"We should go for lunch," she said. "There's a cute little bistro a block away. I haven't eaten in weeks."

I laughed because it hadn't been that long, but it felt like it. I wasn't sure about sharing a meal with Tricia; she'd probably criticize my order. But she did have the company credit card, and it had been three hours since my last coffee, so I agreed.

"Great, you should order the Cornish hen. It is simply to die for," she said, and I tried not to roll my eyes.

When we got to the restaurant, I was pleasantly surprised by the ambience. I expected it to be some stuffy restaurant with a snobby maître d' and menus printed in French only. Yes, I lived in a bilingual country, but I'd barely got by in my French classes. Instead, the restaurant had blue mosaic floor tiles with pink-painted walls, and a white-knit tapestry hung from the ceiling. It was a cute, boho-chic bistro with an eclectic style that instantly made me feel comfortable and cozy.

After a few minutes of perusing the menu, the waiter came to take our orders.

"What can I get for you, mademoiselle?" he asked me.

"I'll have the burger with poutine," I said.

Tricia raised her eyes above the menu and then shook her head.

"And for you, madam?" the server asked Tricia.

"I'll have your specialty, the Cornish hen," she replied.

"A great choice, madam."

I silently grumbled at the waiter for not congratulating my choice, but I conceded. I would be the bigger person here.

"So, how do you know about this place?" I asked.

"I come here with Jill all the time. It's one of our favorite spots," she said. Jill Jackson was the host of the biggest daytime talk show in Canada—*The Morning Show*. Tricia constantly name-dropped her celebrity friends and I admit it had started to rattle me.

She took a sip of her water and looked around the room. Maybe she was looking for a better lunch date, and frankly so was I. Tricia and I made fantastic work partners, but we were terrible friends.

"You should network more, you know. Get to more parties, meet more people, start to build a name for yourself," she emphasised this last part.

"I think I go to enough parties and I'm meeting the right amount of people," I said looking right at her, and then I grabbed my own glass to sip some water.

She took a long look at me, and my shoulders slouched a bit under her gaze. She opened her mouth, like she was about to say something, but then took a big breath and looked away. I narrowed my eyes at her because she was acting strange. She struggled to avoid my eyes.

"When I was twenty-one-years old, I landed an internship at the Alderman Agency," she said, still not looking at me, and took another sip from her glass.

"Really? I didn't know that you worked at such a large firm. You never mentioned it."

"And after today, I never will again. Do you understand?"

"Yes, of course. What happened?"

"I was a real go-getter back then."

I was about to laugh because did she really think she was no longer a go-getter? But I contained my mirth when I realized she was serious.

"I worked every night until midnight and every weekend too. I volunteered at all the events and even created a few during my free time. I was excited to be in PR and no one was going to slow me down."

She fidgeted with her fingers and took another sip of her water to keep them busy.

"One of the execs took an interest in me. He would let me in on some new client information and show me some of his presentations for my feedback. I was reeling from being singled out and shown such preference."

I nodded. I didn't want to interrupt her.

"Well, I stayed late one night at work. Everyone had left the office, but I stuck around to finish a presentation on an event I wanted to propose to one of the clients. Ji...The exec called me into his office, said there was something he wanted me to take a look at."

I could tell from her tone that it wasn't going to be a PowerPoint slide.

"When I got inside his office, he waved me over to his computer. Me, being model-like tall, I had to bend down to see what he was trying to show me and that's when he, well, he put his hand on me."

My eyes grew bigger, but I kept quiet.

"I was shocked and didn't move a muscle. I didn't know what to do or how to react. I think he may have mistaken that as an invitation to move forward. He then stood up and tried to kiss me, but I pulled back. He told me not to be a tease. I told him I wasn't interested in him like that. He said he knew I liked older men and not to be coy about it. I had mentioned that in passing but assured him I did not want to have relationships with people in the office."

She took another sip of her water.

"He got angry and said I was naïve, said it happened all the time. He may have been right, but I knew I didn't want one with him. He tried to make another move and I reacted and pushed him down. That's when he got angry and lost it. He screamed at me to get out. He said I was finished, and I would never work in PR again."

Her voice got softer.

"He tried his hardest to make good on this promise. He got me fired, saying I stole his ideas for my presentation. He said I stole products from the brand shelves and that I passed along company information to competing agencies. He covered his bases to ruin me. Me being an intern and he an executive, I was let go right away and never given any references. I had a hell of a time finding another internship, and then a job, because he made sure to repeat his lies to any PR agency that would listen. You know how we love to gossip."

I nodded.

"Anyhow, I decided to work at a television station and networked there until I landed other PR jobs through my media references. It made me realize that I needed to not only do the work but take credit for it. I needed to fight for myself and for my professional integrity. I could not rely on others to pat me on the back. I needed to reach out and grab it for myself. Because sleazeballs like him couldn't hurt me if I had built myself up."

"It wasn't your fault, Tricia," I said.

"I know that. But I shouldn't have allowed him to take me down like that."

"You had no part in his scheme. It wasn't your fault," I repeated.

Her eyes connected with mine for a few seconds, but she looked away.

"Anyway, I told you this to explain why I'm so hard on you. You are very good, Michaela, but you are leaving yourself vulnerable to an attack."

"An attack?"

"Yes, a professional attack. You don't stand up for yourself and you hope that people will just take note of your work and reward you for it," she said.

"Well, I did ask for my title to be promoted," I reminded her.

"Yes, after I was given the same one in a third of the time that it took you to get yours. You should have been given your title at least a year ago. You need to make clear what you do, and demand what you want. No one is going to give you anything in this world."

"Is that why you told Suzanne that it was your idea to put the client's logo behind the bar at the Hugo Boss party?" I stared straight into her eyes and dared her to deny it. I heard it from Suzanne herself.

"I did not tell Suzanne it was my idea. I told her it was a great idea and pointed to the logo at the bar." She made a motioning gesture with her hand. "It was so loud in there. She must have thought I was taking credit for it."

"Well, that's convenient for you. How about the Four Seasons stunt you pulled?" I asked.

"Oh no, that was for your own good. That taught you a valuable lesson. Trust no one—always check things out for yourself. If you are going to rely on other people, you better be ready to accept their mistakes, as well. I knew the lobby bar was open, but you didn't. You needed to confirm it for yourself."

"Huh, that's true. I do say half of my job is making sure everyone else is doing theirs. I should take my own advice."

"Exactly."

The waiter arrived at that moment with our lunch.

"And the Cornish hen, was that a test for me to make my own decisions?"

"No, when it comes to food, I never lie. On that one, you should have listened to me."

I inhaled the delicious aroma from the Cornish hen and my mouth watered. Darn it, she was right—I should have gotten the hen.

"You know, Tricia, you don't need to test me anymore. We can be friends now."

She cut off a piece of her hen and brought it to her mouth. "Sometimes friends don't make the best business partners. Let's not ruin a good thing here."

I smiled and took a bite of my burger.

Yup, should have gotten the hen.

Twelve

Michaela

The next day was Saturday and I decided to spend the entire day catching up on sleep. If there was time, I'd binge a few TV series and then maybe do some cleaning. Well, two out of three wasn't bad. By four o'clock, I was on season one, episode ten of *Rags to Runway*.

"No, you have to tell Kara you slept with her boyfriend!" I shouted at the TV screen. "Don't be that girl! Tell her!"

Dev had recommended the series to me. He said I'd get a kick out of the PR stunts. I cringed at a few scenes, especially when one designer painted his logo on a rival's entire clothing collection the night before the runway show." He had called it branding, I would call it a PR nightmare.

There were only five minutes left in the episode when my phone beeped with a text. I picked it up and saw it was from Tricia.

Tricia: OMG guess who I ran into last night?

Me: I don't know. Who?

Tricia: Tim. The sales exec from yesterday's client presentation

Me: What!? Where? How?

Tricia: Well, I was at this party...you know, NETWORKING. when who walks through the door but the tall handsome blond from the meeting

Me: Oh yes, I know who you're talking about now. He is cute. Did you go up to him?

Tricia: Hell no, I waited for him to come up to me. We need to show them they need us, not the other way around

Me: Thank you, oh wise one

Tricia: Don't be snide, it isn't attractive on you

Me: Stop stalling and tell me if he said anything about the meeting and our chances

Tricia: Well, he said we caused quite a debate after we left

Me: Really? Is that a good thing or a bad thing?

Tricia: He wouldn't say, just that he thinks we still have a great chance of getting the account even though a few of the execs didn't agree with our approach. But he said others were really impressed

Me: Ugh, so we still have no idea

Tricia: Nope. But I did get his number

Me: lol, good for you

Tricia: [high five emoji]

I was still smiling when I put my phone down and warmed up a bag of microwave popcorn. As the kernels popped, I heard another text come in. Thinking it was probably Tricia congratulating herself on the intel, I left it to reply later.

However, when I got back to the couch and picked up my phone, I noticed it wasn't from Tricia. The text was from Hunter. I didn't see the message on my screen, just his name.

How did he get my number? Wait, I remembered programming it into his phone when we were on our date. I thought myself so cute and clever at the time. I regretted that decision. I swiped up the screen and opened my new text message.

Hunter: Michaela, I know you must be surprised to see a message from me after how things ended between us.

Um, yes, that's exactly what I was thinking. Then, another message came through.

Hunter: So much has happened since I last saw you. So much is now at stake. I understand if you never want to see me again, but I'm begging you, please hear me out. Let me explain.

Me: What's happened? Is everyone ok?

Hunter: No. But I'd rather tell you everything in person. Can I see you?

Me: You are going to fly all the way from New York to Toronto just to have a conversation with me? This must be serious

Hunter: It is.

Me: Ok, if that's what you want. When are you planning to make the trip?

Hunter: Now

Wow, he was not kidding. That only gave me a few hours to get myself ready.

Me: Do you want to meet at a bar? I know a good one close to my apartment.

Hunter: I'd rather meet at your apartment if that's alright with you. We need to talk and probably won't be able to do that at a bar.

My apartment. Was I sure I wanted to have Hunter in my apartment? I didn't know if I could have him so close to me and not dive into his arms. But he was right; we wouldn't hear each other at a bar.

Me: Ok, my apartment is fine

Hunter: Thank you

Then:

Hunter: You can open the door now

Me: What!! You're here! Now???

Hunter: Yes

He must be joking. He could not be outside my door right now. He couldn't. A knock tapped on the door. *Crap, he really was here.*

"One minute," I shouted at the door and ran to my bathroom. I brushed my teeth and combed the knots out of my hair. I was wearing a tank top and a pair of sweatpants but no bra. I ran to my room and tried to find my bra...ugh, they all needed to be washed. I hadn't had time to do laundry since I got back from New York and I was planning to do it tomorrow. *It's fine*. He was not here for me; he was here because something had happened.

Relax, Michaela, and just be cool.

I walked calmly to the door and looked through the peephole. Oh my, he looked as good as I remembered. Maybe better. His hair was dishevelled now, not perfectly combed as I had suspected he woke up with every morning. I guess I was wrong about a lot of things when it came to Hunter. His full mouth pulled down into a frown and his fingers rubbed the back of his neck.

I opened the door and took a deep breath.

"Hi," I said.

He just stared at me.

"Are you alone?"

"Yes," I said and waved him in. "You don't have to worry about anyone interrupting us."

"Good," he said, and then I was swept into his arms and he kissed me like my lips were medicine to his fever. His face was hot under my palms and his hair got messier as I raked my fingers through it. I held on tight, at first because I wanted to, and then because I needed to, as his passion took my breath away.

"God, I missed you so much," he said.

"I missed you too," I said as his lips moved onto my neck.

"I thought I would never hold you again," he said.

"I thought you never wanted to again."

"I never not wanted you, Michaela. It was never a question of want." His hands curved over my hips. "I will always want you."

"You can't keep saying stuff like that and kissing me like this. It's very confusing." He let go of me and took a step back. He ran his hand through his hair and exhaled.

"You're right, I'm sorry. I just lose control when I see you, but that's no excuse."

"Well, I'm not exactly upset, but I don't understand what's going on. Why are you here?"

"Please sit, Michaela, there's so much we need to discuss. And he really doesn't have much time."

"Who doesn't?"

"My father."

"Is he okay?"

"No. That's why I'm here. There's a lot to explain and very little time."

We were now sitting side by side on my couch and he closed his eyes. I felt like he was buying time to gather up his next words.

"I come from a very distinct group of people."

"Okay. Like a specific culture or region?" I asked.

"Not exactly. We are similar to you in many ways, but quite different in others. You see, we have certain characteristics that may scare some people, so we keep it a secret. That's why I can't tell you exactly what I am."

"You're not making sense, Hunter. Do you have secret piercings? Rituals? Whatever it is, you can tell me."

"I can't. It is one of the rules of my people, we cannot disclose who we are. It is the most important rule. One I cannot break."

"Okay, fine. What does this have to do with me? Why are you here now?"

"Two days ago, someone tried to kill my father."

My mouth hung open, but I said nothing because I wanted him to go on.

"Someone poisoned him in his sleep, but he managed to sputter most of it out. He lives, but barely, and we do not know for how much longer."

"Hunter, that's terrible. I'm so sorry."

"The physician is trying to develop an antidote, but I cannot rely solely on this, as he may not be able to make one in time. My father's youngest sister, my aunt Olympia, said something that brought me running here to you."

"What did she say?"

He reached for my face. "She told me to find the one with the violet eyes," he said, caressing my eyebrow and the skin around my temple.

"Why?"

"She thinks you can save him."

We were staring at each other, face-to-face now. I blinked, incredulously. "Why would she think that? How could I possibly save your father? I don't have a medical degree."

"When she was a child, she overheard her grandmother speak of a woman with violet eyes. She said this woman was the only one who could save her sister."

"Maybe there was some doctor with purple eyes in her town, or maybe someone with purple eyes worked at an apothecary and concocted some potent remedies. Whatever it was, it has nothing to do with me. I'm sorry Hunter, I can't save your father."

He continued to stare at me, and I held his gaze. "From the moment I met you, there was a connection between us. There is something special about you, Michaela. I feel it here." He held the palm of my hand up to his heart.

"I feel it too, Hunter, but not because I'm some magical being that can miraculously save a man from imminent death. I feel it as a woman feels an attraction toward a man."

"There is more than just attraction between us," he said.

I smiled. "So, you admit there's an attraction between us."

He raised his eyebrow and looked back at the hallway where we'd been pawing at each other a few minutes ago. "Attraction has never been the problem."

I couldn't help but grin.

"I've never felt it as intensely with anyone else as I do with you. Why do you think that is?"

"Um, well, maybe because there's something special between us. Maybe it's something we should explore?"

"I think this is more than just physical attraction. I think there's something else at play, something beyond just me and you."

"That's a lot of pressure early on in a relationship, Hunter."

"Tell me this. How many people are in your family?"

"I told you, it was just my parents and me."

"I meant beyond your immediate family. You mentioned an aunt. Anyone else? Other aunts, uncles, or cousins?"

"No. There's no one else. Why?"

"Does anyone else you know have violet eyes?"

"Why? Do you want to go and kiss them?"

He looked at me like he didn't appreciate my humor. Well, I didn't appreciate him denying what we had.

"Answer the question. Please," he said.

"Yes. I got them from my mother, and she got them from her mother. Seems like the recessive gene is passed along the maternal side of the family."

"And this aunt of yours, is she still alive? I'm sorry to bring it up, I know you lost your parents, and this is difficult for you."

I appreciated him saying that, and for that reason I responded. "Yes, she lives in the suburbs, about thirty minutes from here."

"Do you think she may know something about the power of the violet eyes?"

"They don't have any powers, trust me! I've been seeing through them for twenty-six years and I haven't lasered anyone or seen through walls."

"Do you think you could take me to her? See if maybe she knows more than you do?"

"Are you serious?"

"Yes. My father's life is at stake."

Having wished I could have done something to save my parents, anything to have had more time with them, I relented and agreed to take him. "Okay, let me call her and see if she's available tomorrow."

"Tonight."

"Pushy, aren't you?"

"She may not have any information, so I need to know as soon as possible."

"Okay, but I haven't spoken to her in weeks," I said and wondered if it had been more like months. "How do I spring that I need to see her tonight?"

"She's family, Michaela, and family always makes time for each other."

I got a little flustered by this. *Family*. I hadn't felt part of a family in a very long time. I didn't know what it meant to be the most important person in someone's life, to have someone put everything in their life down if I asked it of them. Would Aunt Julie do that for me? Maybe Hunter was right, maybe she would.

"Okay, I'll call her." I picked up my cell phone and dialed Aunt Julie's number. I hit the call button before I changed my mind.

Aunt Julie picked up after three rings.

"Michaela, is that you, sweetie?"

"Hi, Aunt Julie. Yes, it's me. How are you?"

"I'm good, dear. It's so great to hear from you. How's work going?"

"It's going really well." I paused and then took a deep breath. "Aunt Julie, would it be all right if I came over tonight? I mean, if you're not busy."

"Yes, of course. Is everything okay?"

"Yes, I'm okay. I just have some questions that can't wait. And I'm bringing a friend, sorry to spring this all on you."

"Don't apologize, dear. I'm happy to have you and any friend you wish to bring. I'll see you soon."

"Thanks, Aunt Julie. See you soon."

I ended the call and looked at Hunter.

"Huh, that was easier than I thought. You may be right about this family thing." He smiled and headed toward the front door.

"Ready?" he asked.

"No. Look at me," I said and pointed to my ensemble. The heat in his eyes made me blush. "Give me five minutes to get dressed."

"All right," he said. As I raced to my bedroom door, his voice stopped me. "And Michaela?"

"Yes, Hunter," I called out as I entered the bedroom.

"Lock your door."

I smiled as I closed the bedroom door and locked it.

Thirteen

Michaela

I plugged Aunt Julie's home address into the navigation system after getting into Hunter's rental car. Hunter drove while I fidgeted in the passenger seat. I strummed my fingers on the door handle. I was nervous. About twenty minutes into the drive, I noticed familiar neighborhoods and storefronts. The sights took me back nearly ten years to when I'd lived here. Memories flashed before me.

I remembered my dad driving us into the city to visit the Royal Ontario Museum, or to see the Christmas windows on Queen Street, or when they took me skating at Nathan Phillips Square. I would never forget the drives back because I always pretended to sleep in the back seat. I would sneak a peek and see Dad holding Mom's hand over the stick shift. At the time I felt awkward with their displays of affection. What I wouldn't give now to see Dad grab Mom for a hug or spin her around the kitchen table.

The navigation system showed seven more minutes to our destination, but I knew it was at least ten from the high school we'd just passed.

"You're quiet," Hunter said.

"I'm thinking"

"What are you thinking about?"

"How I never appreciated what I had until it was gone."

"Yes, we can all relate to that. I thought my dad would be around for most of my life."

"He's still alive. The physician is working on an antidote. There's still hope, Hunter."

He looked at me and smiled. "Yes, there's still hope."

Hunter pulled onto my old street and bent his head forward to look for the house numbers.

"It's the red brick one down there." I pointed to my old house. It still looked very much like it did when I lived there. Aunt Julie travelled so much when she was younger, she'd never needed to buy a home; she'd always stayed with us when she was in town. After my parents died, she stayed to raise me and has been here ever since.

"Are you ready?" Hunter asked.

I breathed deeply. "Yes."

He reached over and gave my hand a squeeze. "You can do this."

I smiled back, gave him a brisk nod, and stepped out of the car. The plain white doorbell looked the same too. I rang it and waited. When I peeked through the window, Aunt Julie was rushing toward us.

"Michaela, sweetheart," she said and reached in to give me a huge hug. It felt so good to be held by Aunt Julie. I wrapped my arms around her and squeezed back. She let go, looked at Hunter and then back to me.

"Oh, Aunt Julie, this is Hunter Durand, the friend I told you about."

"Very nice to meet you, Hunter. Won't you both come in?"

"The pleasure is mine Ms..."

I just realized I'd never told Hunter my mom's maiden name, but Aunt Julie took care of that real quick. "Shedley. But please, call me Julie."

"I see Michaela's beauty comes from her mom's side of the family."

"Oh, your charm will get you far in this house, Hunter." She laughed and walked us to the family room. Just like the outside, the inside of the home so far looked exactly as I remembered it. I wondered if Aunt Julie liked the décor or was too sentimental to take it down. I suspected the latter.

The family room had the same light brown velour sofas, a beige carpet and two side tables with silver lamps on top. The framed family photos were still up, and I avoided looking at them.

"Can I get you both some coffee or tea, perhaps?" my aunt asked.

Hunter glanced at me to respond first. "I'll have coffee," I said.

"Same for me, thank you."

She must have had a pot prepared before we arrived because it didn't take her long to come out with a tray of coffee and freshly baked cake. Mmm, I missed that smell.

We sat with our coffee and cake. No one said a word. Hunter kept looking my way—if only his eyes could talk. I decided to break the ice, as I could tell he was waiting for me to take the lead.

"Aunt Julie, thank you for seeing us on such short notice," I began.

"Anytime, dear. You can come back home and visit anytime you wish," she said.

"Thank you. While I am glad to be here, we did come with a purpose in mind. We are here to find out if there's any information you can give us."

"Okay, you mentioned on the phone there were some questions you wanted to ask me," she replied.

I glanced at my aunt Julie's eyes; they were brown, not purple. I didn't know where to begin and I was unsure what I was supposed to ask her. So, I said the first thing that popped into my head.

"Hunter thinks I have magical powers because I have purple eyes." There, I'd said it.

"What?" she asked.

Hunter straightened out on the sofa and gave me an exasperated look.

"That's not exactly what I said," he explained. "Ms...I mean, Julie.

I understand Michaela got her unusual eye color from her mother, and her grandmother as well, is that correct?"

"Yes," she said and chuckled. "I remember being upset when I was a child because I wanted eyes like my mother too. But I remember my mother saying that we all have beauty within, it doesn't matter what color our outside is."

Hunter smiled. "I'm wondering if she ever mentioned anything else in your presence about her family. Did they live here in Toronto, as well?"

"My parents were immigrants. They came from Italy shortly after they married and had my sister, Lucia, a year after that. It was just the four of us."

"Italy, mmm, Shedley does not sound Italian," said Hunter.

"It doesn't, but that can be the case, especially in the north with so many countries bordering the northern provinces."

"That's true." He seemed more convinced. "Did your mother ever speak of her homeland?"

"She did, and we visited Italy once, but we never went back to her hometown. She said it brought her too many memories of the people she'd left behind."

"Mmm...perhaps...or maybe not," he whispered this last part, but I still heard it. What was he getting at?

"Can you remember your mother saying or doing anything unusual during your childhood?"

"She was an immigrant mother living in Canada—most of what she did was unusual to my younger self," said Aunt Julie with a grin. "I think my sister had it the hardest. She was four years older than me, and my mother made her stay in and study old textbooks while my father took me to the park or a ball game."

"And did your sister ever mention anything strange to you?"

"No, Lucy, never mentioned those extra study lessons to me, and of course I never brought them up. I didn't want her to think I had an interest in reading them."

"Is there anything else you can remember? Anything you would now think strange about your parents?" asked Hunter.

"Not really," she explained. "They kept to themselves, didn't socialize with any of the neighbors or join any committees. They would best be described as recluses. I do remember my mother getting very upset with my sister for being social, for doing things in the community and getting recognition for it."

She brought her finger to her mouth and tapped her lips.

"There was this one time when Lucy held a protest at our high school to boycott a particular politician that was visiting. Lucy's name was featured on the front page of The Star and I thought my mother would lose her mind. She went crazy, shouting, 'Do you know what this means? What have you done?' I thought she was worried about Lucy not getting into college with a bad reputation, but I don't think that was it. Now that I think about it, I do recall Lucy saying she couldn't live like her, that she wouldn't be a recluse. I remember my mother telling her she had to, that she had no choice. I thought that was strange. Mmm, I haven't thought about that day in a very long time."

"Do you think your sister kept those textbooks she was studying all those years ago?" asked Hunter. He leaned forward to the edge of the couch, his hands pressed together, prayerlike, in front of his lips.

"If she did, they would be in the storage room in the basement. She had tons of boxes down there. I always said I would go through them and give the stuff away to Goodwill, but I haven't had the heart to do it."

"Do you mind if Michaela and I go through them?" asked Hunter.

"Of course not, if that's how you wish to spend your Saturday night."

I knew with his father not well, that was exactly how Hunter planned to spend his Saturday night.

I put my hand on his shoulder and slid it down until our fingers intertwined. I pulled him up from the couch and led him toward the basement stairs.

Fourteen

Michaela

We had been going through the boxes for hours. At one point, Aunt Julie brought us sandwiches and soda, God bless her. Hunter hardly ate a thing. He seemed consumed by the thought that he would find something here.

I didn't know what to feel. On one hand, I knew there was nothing mysterious about my past, and on the other, I wanted us to find something that could save his father. I worried we were only wasting our time down in the basement, until I stumbled across something.

"Hunter, come take a look at this," I said.

He dropped the box he was rummaging through and walked over to where I was standing.

"What is it?" he asked.

"It's my old teddy bear, Roxy."

"Oh, that's sweet. Was he one of your favorites?"

"Yes, that's why it's so strange that he's here. When I was twelve, my mother told me she'd given him away during one of her annual spring-cleaning binges. She said she'd got rid of a bunch of my baby stuff and didn't think I wanted him anymore. I was devastated. I told her she was mistaken and that I loved Roxy. She smiled and said she was sure one day he would find a way back to me. And now, here he is. What do you think this means?"

"I think it means she wanted you to find him here, after she was gone."

I pursed my lips and looked at Roxy as if he were a ghost. I finally picked up the bear and turned him around to see if there were any scuffs or damage.

"He looks to be in mint condition," said Hunter.

"Yes, that's the problem."

"It is?"

"When I was seven, I put Roxy down on top of the deck. When I went to get him—his arm must have been caught on a nail—because I pulled and tore a bit of the seam. My mother wanted to sew him back up, but I refused. I said Roxy had already been through enough and we should just bandage him up. She agreed and so he remained torn and unsewn until the last day I saw him."

"Well, it looks like someone sewed him back up. You know what you're going to have to do?" asked Hunter.

I did, but I still hesitated. I finally pushed my fingernail into the seam that had once been ripped and tore it open. *I'm so sorry, Roxy.*

I carefully rummaged through the stuffing as though Roxy could feel my invasive fingers. I didn't feel anything at first, but then my finger touched a hard object. I pulled it out through the open seam. It was a key.

"Huh, I wonder what this opens up?" I asked.

"I don't know, but we need to find out," said Hunter. Motivated into action, he moved boxes out of the way and pushed the dresser that Roxy had been sitting on away from the wall.

"Wait," I said. "What's that?"

In the darkest corner of the room, there was an outline of a door.

"I never knew that was there," I said.

Hunter turned to me with his palm wide open, waiting for me to pass him the key.

I hesitated. I had this terrible feeling that whatever was behind the door was something that would change me forever. I didn't know if I was ready for it.

"Michaela, please." Hunter's eyes looked hopeful.

This wasn't just about me, though—a man's life was on the line. So, I handed Hunter the key.

He opened the door, but it was too dark inside. I couldn't see a thing. At least, *I* couldn't see anything, but Hunter walked directly into the room and located a light bulb off to the side. He pulled on what I presumed was a string, and the light bulb turned on. The room was tiny. Hunter and I barely fit inside. There were two large trunks, one stacked on top of the other. Hunter tried to lift the lid, but it was locked with a numerical security code.

Hunter turned to me. "When is your birthday?"

"July 27, 1997," I said. He tried a combination of those numbers to unlock the code.

"No, that's not it."

"Try my mom's birthday. August 3, 1965," I suggested.

After a few seconds, he shook his head.

Think, Michaela. What could it be?

"Oh wait, try this. August 1, 2000."

He punched in those numbers.

"Yes! That's it!" he said. "Whose birthday is that? Your father's? Julie's?"

I smiled. "No, that's Roxy's birthday."

He laughed, "Of course. Good thinking."

Hunter opened the first trunk and inside were large leather-bound tomes, at least a dozen of them. We opened up a book and flipped through the pages together. The book was written in what appeared to me to be Italian, but not modern-day Italian. I had a difficult time reading and understanding any of the sentences. I really should have paid more attention to my *nonna* when she'd tried to teach me the language.

"Can you make these out?" I asked Hunter. "My rudimentary Italian isn't helpful."

"They seem to be history texts, but my Italian is limited to today's modern language."

I nodded and continued to look through the pages. "This one here has a map," I said and passed Hunter the book to show him. The map mainly focused on Italy and northern Africa.

He looked at it for a few minutes but then shook his head. "I'm not sure what this is about," he said. "Let's see what's in the other trunk." He punched in Roxy's birthday code, and it worked on this trunk too.

Inside there were more texts but also some yellowing, old-looking papers, bound together with a string. There were two grey robes that I pulled out and inspected.

"Wow, these look like something a druid would wear," I said and held the garments up against my body.

"Yes, they do," said Hunter as he reached out to touch the fabric. "And I think they're quite old. This fabric feels like something made at least two hundred years ago."

"Are you a historian now?" I laughed. He shook his head and simply said, "No, I'm not."

"Well, I guess my parents liked a little cosplay," I joked, hoping to lighten his mood. It didn't work. "Hey, it looks like we're not going to get very far with this stuff tonight. Aunt Julie says she's made up the guest rooms for us. Why don't we call it a night and then try again tomorrow with a fresh pair of eyes? Maybe we take some of these books to the university to see if someone there can translate them? I have a friend in the Italian department at the University of Toronto."

"You should go up and get some rest. I will stay and spend a bit more time looking through these trunks. I feel like we're close, and I won't be able to get any sleep anyway," he said, but he wasn't looking at me. He was skimming through the papers.

I crouched down to where he was sitting on the storage room

floor and kissed his cheek. He reached out and held my face with his hands. He stared into my eyes for what felt like forever and then moved closer to press his lips to mine. The kiss was soft and sweet. He took his time kissing my top lip and then gently sucking on my bottom one. He pulled away slowly but still held me when he said, "I feel like there's something here, Michaela. Not just something that will save my father, but something that will help us too. There's something extraordinary about you. I can feel it."

"Well, I've always known that about myself Hunter, it's taken you long enough to realize it."

I smiled and despite him trying to hold it back, a soft smile broke upon his face.

Fifteen

Michaela

Hunter was fighting an attacker. His amber eyes glowed and his muscles bunched through the fabric of his clothes. His movements were unnaturally fast and unquestionably lethal. Hunter punched the other man in the gut causing the man to bounce up and off the ground. Hunter's face frightened me, as though I saw him through some sort of animal filter. His eyes were wild, and his teeth were bared like he was ready to go for the man's jugular.

I called out his name, "Hunter!" But he didn't hear me. I screamed it and he finally looked back at me. Even though he was looking at me, he didn't seem to recognize me.

Was this even Hunter?

He resumed his fight, but I was horrified to see the attacker had a knife. He lifted the weapon, ready to stab Hunter with it. I screamed again to warn him, but Hunter kicked the knife away with one leg and then with the other kicked the attacker in the face. He hit him so hard the man fell to the ground. Hunter put his foot on the man's throat and turned to glare at me.

I shouted, "No, don't do it," but he didn't let up. Instead, he pushed his foot into the man's throat harder.

"No," I shouted again.

This time, when Hunter looked at me, something in his face changed. He stared into my eyes and his feral ones looked afraid. He looked scared—of me.

"Michaela," he said.

"Yes, Hunter, it's me," I shouted back.

Michaela.

Michaela.

"Michaela, wake up."

It was Hunter's voice again, but we weren't in danger. He was shaking my shoulders. That was only a dream. Oh, thank God.

"Michaela, are you all right? I heard you shouting."

"Yes, I'm okay. It was just a bad dream."

"What was it about?"

"You."

He raised his eyebrows, "And that makes it a bad dream?"

"Yes, well, never mind. I really don't want to talk about it."

"All right," he said and kept staring at me.

"So, are we heading to the university today?" I asked, trying to change the subject.

"No, we're going to Italy."

"What? What are you talking about?"

"Get ready and I'll explain over breakfast," he said.

I showered, dressed, and made my way to the kitchen. Aunt Julie and Hunter were already seated at the table.

"Good morning, dear. I hope you had a good rest," my aunt greeted me.

"Yes, thank you," I mumbled and tried to forget the dream. There were eggs, toast, and bacon spread out on the table. It all looked so good, I dug in.

"So, what's this about Italy?" I asked through a mouthful of eggs.

"Last night as I was going through the texts and papers, I found some letters," explained Hunter. "Your mother corresponded with a woman named Anna Maria Tassone. In the last letter, Anna Maria told her she was needed back at the village immediately and to bring her tools," he said.

I nodded and spread some butter on my toast.

"There's something else, Michaela," he said. "The letter was dated March 22, 2008, one month before your parents' plane went down over the Adriatic Sea."

I stopped eating. I stopped moving altogether.

"I think your parents were not just vacationing. I think they went to Italy on a mission," Hunter said with urgency in his voice. "She referred to your mother having tools. I need to know what those were. They may be the key to saving my father."

I stared at my aunt Julie. "Did you know about this?"

She shook her head. "No, she just told me she was going to travel Europe with your dad. I never questioned her. They travelled together for research all the time."

"Yes, they did travel a lot," I said. "And they always told me it was for research."

"I don't think it had anything to do with research," said Hunter.

"Why would they lie to us?" asked Aunt Julie, directing the question to Hunter. "My God, do you think they were killed?"

She'd asked the question that was burning in my heart but I couldn't find the strength to say out loud.

"I don't know," said Hunter in a low voice. "But we are going to that village and getting some answers. There's a flight tonight at 8:00 p.m."

"Tonight? I have to let work know. I have vacation time, but this isn't much notice." I said, knowing that I had to go. If my parents' death was more than accidental, I needed to find out.

"I'll call Suzanne on our way back to my apartment. I need to head home to pack."

Hunter dug into his breakfast now that he had shared his news. I couldn't eat another bite.

***

Suzanne took the news well. It seemed she was still riding off the

New York high, so she let me get away with a short-notice vacation. She told me to network while I was there, that she'd love to have Gucci as a client. I didn't know where she thought I was going, but I was sure this tiny village in Italy wouldn't have many designers living there.

The airplane was full; I had no idea how Hunter got two tickets on this flight. I didn't bother to ask either. I was too preoccupied with the fact that I was flying first-class.

"You will not get any sleep if you keep bouncing on your seat like that," said Hunter.

"I can't help it—I'm too excited to sleep."

"You've flown before, haven't you?"

"Yes, but I've only walked past the larger seats to get to my economy one and was later shooed away from the curtain when trying to use the bathroom. This is the first time I've actually sat in first class." I may have squealed when I said the last part.

He laughed at my giddiness.

"Oh, and I've never been to Italy either."

"You said your parents travelled there before, isn't that right?"

"They did, but I never went with them. When I was younger, I was told I would appreciate it more when I got older. When I got older, I was told it was more important to get a summer job and learn responsibility. They promised to take me when I finished high school before beginning university. But then...well, it didn't happen. And I didn't want to go after they were gone. I knew it would only remind me of them."

"I know this is difficult for you, Michaela. And I know you are doing this for me. I don't know how to thank you."

"As much as I'd love to have you indebted to me, I admit it's not just for you. I want to be there if you find out anything about my parents. Also, I'm glad that the first time I get to visit Italy, I'm here with someone I can lean on."

"Michaela, you can depend on me. I will always be by your side if you need me."

As much as I loved my independence, it felt good to depend on someone when I needed it. I put my head on his shoulder and wrapped my arm around his.

"You seem to be in a better mood this morning," I said as I made myself more comfortable.

"I am," he said. "I spoke to Thomas before we boarded, and he said my father is stable and his heart seems strong. The physician feels confident he can keep him this way until they can get the antidote ready, or we return with something more."

"That's really great news, Hunter," I said and felt relieved his father was out of immediate danger.

"It also helps having a pretty girl like you holding on to me," he said and reached for my free hand.

"Hunter?"

"Mmm?"

"I think I'm falling for you."

He didn't say anything. I didn't really expect him to say it back, but I wanted him to know how I felt. And then I heard him say, softly...

"I've already fallen."

Sixteen

Michaela

I'd only been in Italy for two hours and I was convinced I'd met the world's worst taxi driver. He shouted at every driver who passed him, waving his arm furiously out the window. Stop signs were only a suggestion to him, and he used his horn as a warning that he was about to break some traffic law so move out of his way.

We'd been in his car for more than an hour and I was holding on to Hunter's knee and the door handle when he turned to Hunter and said, *"Siamo qui."*

"Michaela, we're here," Hunter translated for me.

"Oh, thank God we've made it here alive."

Hunter smiled and paid the driver while I got our suitcases from the trunk. The trunk was locked, so I knocked on the car to get the driver's attention.

"Stai attenta," he shouted and walked back to open the trunk.

Hunter joined us and helped with the bags. We had barely taken a step back when the car took off and left us in its dust. I wiped my mouth. I didn't enjoy the irony of that turn of phrase.

I looked around and, for the first time, really took Italy in. Earlier, I was terrified of taking my eyes off the road, so I didn't get a chance to enjoy the views.

I thought my mom was from northern Italy, but whomever she'd corresponded with lived here in the south. We were in a little village called Gioiosa in Reggio, Calabria. We stood in front of a stone apartment building, maybe three or four stories. On each floor, there were balconies with red-painted railings and clothes left hanging to dry.

The street was narrow—a big SUV would probably take up most of the space between the buildings. The cobblestoned path twisted and turned into other streets leading to more of these quaint buildings.

An older woman in the building across the road sat on her balcony staring at us. I waved my hand to say hello. She didn't wave back or move at all; she just stared. Two little boys were kicking a soccer ball two doors down from us. I raised my hand to wave at them but snapped it back down. I didn't want to risk another rejection. It would be humiliating in front of the older woman.

"Is this our Airbnb?" I asked Hunter while he searched for a key underneath the entrance mat. He found it and beamed up at me.

"Yes. Our host Domenico said he would come by later this evening to ensure we've settled in."

"He just left the key under the mat where anyone would find it?" I asked.

Hunter looked up and behind me to the older woman. "I think they have pretty good security around here. The owner would be instantly notified of any suspicious intruders."

Hunter opened the door and we went inside. Like the street, the inside hallway was narrow and tiled with terracotta stone. The white concrete walls looked as though they had been freshly painted, and the drapes were a beautiful white frothy material that billowed at the bottom. There was a kitchen on the left-hand side and two bedrooms and a washroom down the hallway.

Hunter put my suitcases down in the bedroom closest to the washroom.

"Two bedrooms?" I asked with one snarky eyebrow raised.

"Yes," Hunter said and took an unnecessarily long time arranging my bags in the room.

"You can stay with me, you know," I said in a low voice. I placed my hand on his biceps and turned him toward me. The muscles felt tense under my fingertips.

At first he looked up at the ceiling. Then, he took a breath and stared down into my eyes.

"Michaela, there is nothing I want more, believe me, than to lie on that bed next to you."

"But..." I said, knowing there had to be more.

"But...I don't trust myself enough to stop," he said.

"I'm not asking you to," I told him. "Hunter, you are not my first, and..." and then a thought popped into my head, and I blurted out "Would I be your first?"

He smiled and shook his head. "Not in the way you're thinking, but I've never been with anyone like you. I'm not afraid of making love to you. I'm afraid that I would hurt you."

He must've noticed the confusion on my face because he pulled me into his arms and held me there, tighter than ever before.

"We are here to find a way to help my father and to discover what happened to your parents. But in addition to all of that, I am here hoping to find some information that will lead me to believe that we can be together. That you can be mine and I can be yours, and we can give in to each other as much as we both desire."

He took a deep breath and held me tighter.

"Trust me, I want that as much as I want my father to live. Perhaps more,"

He whispered this last part—perhaps it was meant for just himself. But I heard him, and I heard the anguish in his voice. He held himself back from saying more. I wanted him to tell me but knew better than to push him. So, I stepped back and gave him some space. I would wait patiently until he was ready to spill his secrets.

"You mentioned we aren't searching for the address until tomorrow morning, right?" I asked.

"Yes, I think two strangers showing up unannounced at her doorstep late in the evening would not set us off on the right foot. She probably won't be happy to be disturbed at this hour and may turn us away. Why, what did you have in mind?"

"I noticed there's a beautiful ocean down the street. How about we check it out?" I asked. "I may have packed a bikini when I looked up where we'd be visiting."

He looked down at me and shook his head. "You know it would be torture seeing you in a bikini, right? Sadistically, I don't think I could refuse now that you've mentioned it."

I shooed him out of the room and went in search of the tiniest bathing suit I had.

I may have retreated, but I hadn't lost the battle. Sometimes a soldier's uniform could be the smallest piece of nylon ever stitched.

The beach was only a five-minute walk from our apartment. We followed the cobblestone corridor until it met a sidewalk and found the ocean just across the main street. We had to walk down a ramp nearly ten feet high to get down to the sand.

It was almost five in the afternoon, but the sun was still high in the sky and hot. I took my shoes off so I could feel the sand between my toes.

Oh, that's hot!

I jumped to put my shoes back on, and while Hunter didn't say anything he did have an amused look on his face.

"Don't you laugh," I warned him while holding on to his shoulder for balance to put my shoes back on.

"I wouldn't dare," he replied and then pointed to a section where white chairs and blue umbrellas were laid out on the beach.

"I'll go rent us a couple of chairs," he said and headed toward the cabana. "Pick the ones you want."

It being so late in the evening, I had my pick of chairs and chose two at the front. As I walked closer to the water and our chairs, the sand gave way to tiny pebbles. I placed my bag down on top of the pebbles and sat on one of the chairs. I ventured to remove my shoes again. This time, I only pressed my big toe on the tiny rocks and felt the coolness of the ocean on them. I sighed and sank both feet into the pebbles. The sound of the waves crashing in the ocean beckoned me. The fresh smell of salt and sea filled my nose. I felt so small sitting there before the ocean. The blue water blending in with the blue sky fooled me into thinking I could reach out and touch the ends of the earth. I stretched out my arm in front of me to reach for it.

"Is there someone out there?" Hunter asked as he approached my chair.

I quickly dropped my hand and arched my back.

"Nope, just stretching. I think I'm still stiff from the plane."

"Here, let me rub your shoulders and back," he said, straddling the chair to sit himself behind me. The irony of the sexiest guy I had ever met giving me a back massage, while sitting on a beach in the south of Italy—and I couldn't do anything else about it—was not lost on me.

"What are you smiling about?" he asked.

"Just thinking how this is my perfect fantasy."

"Me too," he said, and I thought I heard a rumble deep in his chest. After a few minutes of enjoying the view and the massage, I stretched my neck from side to side and exhaled.

"Better?" he asked.

"Much," I said and lay down against his chest. Hunter leaned back against the lounge chair and wrapped his arms around me.

"I wasn't kidding. This is beautiful. Something straight out of a dream," I said.

"Do you dream often?" Hunter asked while running his middle finger up and down my arm, raising tiny bumps on my bare flesh.

"I do," I said. "I always have such vivid dreams."

"Tell me about them."

"I dream about work and what I will do when I own my own PR company."

"You will do it. You are very determined. What else?"

I didn't mention the most recent dream I'd had about him nearly killing a man. Somehow, I thought, he may not take that well. So, I stuck to my other dreams.

"I dream about vacations, the ocean, the jungle."

"What do you see when you dream about the jungle?" he asked.

"I see animals roaming around, laying out in the sun. I see a tigress grooming her cubs." I felt him shift underneath me. "I know it's silly. Like, I've never even seen a tiger up close, but I imagine they would take care of their own just like any other parent would."

"Yes, I imagine they would," said Hunter. "What else?"

I didn't speak at first, still staring out into the ocean. "I dream about my parents," I said and felt his arms tighten around me. He didn't say anything, so I went on. "I have the same dream over and over again. I can see my mother far out in the distance and she's speaking to me. I run toward her, but when I reach her it's as if she's on mute. Her mouth is moving but I don't hear a sound. I get so frustrated in my dreams. I'm shouting that I can't hear her, why can't I hear her. I begin to cry, and my mother pulls me into a hug and strokes my hair."

I felt Hunter's fingers in my hair then.

"When I wake up, I swear I can still feel her hands on me. As frustrating as those dreams are, I am thankful for them. But then the realization that I am alone sets in, and I can hardly bear it."

"You are not alone," said Hunter.

"I know I'm not. I have my aunt and my friend Dev. But if I really analyze myself, I think I work in PR because I need to constantly surround myself with people and parties. I don't ever want to feel alone. I think it's my way of guaranteeing there's always a party to plan and people to connect with."

I felt Hunter nod his head behind me. "I like to do what I do because I like to be in control. I like to dominate," he said.

I wanted him to continue so I didn't interrupt, just waited for more.

"But I'm terrified of taking over from my father when my time comes."

"Why? Aren't you already in the family business? Why would it be any different when you take over?" I asked.

"Now I am part of the business—an integral part but still only a member. I uphold all the policies and procedures, but when I'm in charge, then everyone will look to me to make decisions. Don't get me wrong, I have no problem telling people what to do and punishing them if they don't do it. But there's a greater responsibility to being a leader than just adhering to the rules. I would be responsible for not just keeping the status quo but growing our company and ensuring everyone's lives continue to evolve and get better. I want to continue to build what my father and grandfather before me saw—a place where everyone can reach their greatest potential and be productive beings in society. I want to ensure a better life for my...employees."

"Wow, no boss I've ever worked for has had such lofty ambitions. I think you're putting way too much pressure on yourself," I said.

Hunter laughed and put his chin on my head. "You're right. I'm overthinking it. I have to trust that what I've learned has prepared me for my role to come."

"Yes. And if your employees aren't happy, they can leave. No one is forcing them to stay."

"Uh-huh."

I laughed because it sounded like he didn't agree. "What? Are you keeping your employees hostage?"

"No, of course not. It's just that sometimes circumstances keep you where you are. Someone may stay at a job not because they love it but because they were trained for that job and it's what they must do to keep their family together."

"My father was an accountant, and he would tell me that his job wasn't the most exciting one out there but it always put food on the table," I said.

"Yes, sometimes we must do what we are trained for," Hunter said.

"I don't know if I agree with that, or what my father said. Sometimes we have to break free, do something unexpected, do what others would not expect us to do. Maybe then we will truly feel free and be happy. Just because I trained to be a lawyer doesn't mean I have to stick with it for the rest of my life. What if I decide to be an artist instead?"

"That's ridiculous, why would a lawyer want to be an artist? They'd starve."

"What if they don't? What if they become the next Picasso? What if the role we chose when we were just seventeen isn't what we want when we are forty? What if the role that was chosen for us isn't what we are meant to be? What then?"

Hunter didn't say a word.

"We find a way," I whispered. "We find a way to be who we want to be."

I took advantage of Hunter's contemplation to do the unexpected. I jumped out of the chair and pulled off my dress, revealing my black string bikini.

"And right now, I want to be a mermaid,"

I ran into the ocean. I didn't check to see if Hunter followed. I dived in and swam down to the pebbled bottom until I felt my lungs burn. Then I swam back up, breaking through the surface. I gasped and took in a huge gulp of air.

Hunter was there beside me. His hair wet and dripping along the side of his face. He stared at me intently, then dived in, grabbed my waist, and lifted me up onto his shoulders.

I laughed and teetered up top.

"Put me down," I demanded as I wildly kicked my legs against his chest.

"We're going to find a way, Michaela," he said. "Just like you said."

Then he lifted me off his shoulders and slowly slid me down the front of his body. I felt every ridge of his abdomen and every muscle in his arm as I hung on tight. I wrapped my legs around his waist and my arms around his neck.

"Yes, Hunter, we are going to find a way."

I kissed him hard and squeezed every inch of my body against his. The salty ocean clung to his lips. I stood in the middle of the Mediterranean Sea, kissing the most beautiful man I'd ever met. I was terrified of opening my eyes and realizing this was all just a dream.

"Is this real? I'm not dreaming, am I?" I asked.

"You're not dreaming, Michaela."

I sighed and looked up at the sun setting low on the horizon. I didn't know why sunsets made me sad; maybe because they felt like an ending instead of a beginning. I glared at the sun, warning it with my eyes that this was only the beginning. I wouldn't let what Hunter and I felt for each other come to an end.

"Ready to dry off and get some dinner?" asked Hunter. I nodded and gave him one last kiss before jumping down. He grabbed my hand, and we walked toward the shore, turning our backs on the descending sun.

Seventeen

Hunter

In my more than ten decades of life, I've heard and observed many things. There were days I witnessed terrible people committing horrifying acts, which often made me wonder why manticores were considered the monsters and not humans. But today was not one of those days. Today, I saw beauty, experienced optimism, and really understood what it meant to have hope. For the first time, I wanted something badly, and not just for myself but for her, as well.

My whole life, I've lived as a loyal member of my family, a protector of the kingdom, someone who always led by example. But I never asked myself if it was what I truly desired. Today, I realized what I truly want is to love and protect Michaela. Nothing else came close. I didn't know what this union meant for the kingdom, but for the first time, I didn't care. I wanted my father to live, but then I would do what I must to live, as well.

The restaurant Michaela chose was walking distance from the beach. It was a casual spot that made wood oven pizzas and homemade pastas. Michaela ordered the penne alla vodka and I went with the halibut.

"So, where did you learn to speak Italian?" asked Michaela, taking a sip of her white wine.

"Well, I lived in Italy for a short time," I explained, careful not to divulge too much. I wanted to keep it simple yet truthful.

"You did? How come?" she asked with her brilliant smile.

"My family lived in the Middle East for many years, but we needed a change. We moved around to several cities in Europe until we decided to try North America. New York finally felt like home." I took a large bite of my meal, hoping it would encourage her to do the same.

"Wow, I've barely left home. I can't imagine living in so many different cities and learning to speak so many languages," she said.

"To be honest, I speak enough to get by as a tourist. I won't be writing any dissertations in Italian, that's for certain. How about you? I noticed you understand a bit of what is being said around you," I said, attempting to transition the conversation away from my past.

"Yes, my mother would sometimes speak Italian to my father when they wanted to say something in private. I would try to remember the words and then speak into my iPad using Google Translate to figure out what they were talking about."

I laughed out loud because most kids would ignore the conversation, but not Michaela.

"And what did you discover in your translations?" I asked.

"Once they spoke about my grandmother, other times about Egyptian deities and often what they were going to buy me for my birthday or Christmas," she said with a smile. "I always tried to act surprised when I opened the gift, but I'm a terrible liar."

"I can see how you would be a terrible liar. Your face shows every emotion you feel. You'd be a bad poker player too," I said.

"And what am I feeling now?" she asked, with that tempting look in her eyes.

I shook my head and chuckled. When I didn't respond she let it go.

"In all seriousness, I hate liars," she said. "I think that's why I'm feeling unsettled about finding my mother's books. Why didn't she tell me about them?"

"Sometimes people omit the truth to protect the ones they love," I responded, treading carefully.

"No. They omit the truth because they don't want to face the consequences," she replied without hesitation.

My stomach sank and I avoided her searching eyes. It felt like she'd called me out. I omitted the truth to protect my family, my fellow manticores, but she was right. I'd also done it because I was afraid that if Michaela knew what I truly was, she'd walk away. That sounded pathetic, but it was the truth.

"Michaela, you know there are things about me that I cannot reveal to you yet." I wanted her to understand this. "And yes, a part of me is afraid that when you find out, you may not want to be with me."

"I know you're keeping things from me—at least you're honest about that. And I'm trying to be patient until you're ready to tell me, but patience is not one of my virtues. I want you to know, Hunter, there's nothing you could say that would make me not want to be with you," she said. While I knew she meant it, I also knew she could not imagine anything close to the truth.

"I hope you're right," I muttered. My cell phone rang and it was Thomas. "I have to get this. I'll just be a minute." She waved me off and I headed outside. The night air was still warm, and several couples walked up and down the boardwalk. I found a spot between two buildings for more privacy.

I answered the call, "Thomas, it's Hunter. What's happening?"

Michaela

Our conversation left me feeling a bit unsettled. I knew Hunter was keeping things from me. While I understood I had to wait until he was ready to share them, I couldn't shake the feeling that the disclosure would be big. I tried not to overthink it. I didn't want to guess what it could be and set myself into a tailspin. "Love is patient." I would be patient.

I took a large gulp of my wine and finished it. I frowned at the empty glass. It was a lot easier to be patient with wine in my glass.

I spied the waiter, busy with another table, but the bartender looked to be free. Since all my patience was being monopolized by Hunter, I found I had none left for the lack of wine. So, I stood up and decided to carpe diem, or in this case "carpe vino."

The bartender offered me a smooth smile as I walked over with my empty wine glass in hand. When I reached the counter and remembered how terrible my Italian was, I went with the basics.

"Chardonnay *per favore*?" I said and placed my empty wine glass on the bar.

"Certo," said the bartender. He grabbed a bottle of chardonnay and poured me a drink.

"Grazie," I said and turned to walk back to the table. But a man wearing jeans and a crisp white short-sleeved shirt stopped me.

"Ciao," he said with his flashy white smile. He had a medium build, with a dark olive complexion and pale grey eyes. He was strikingly handsome. I couldn't help but notice.

"Ciao," I said and moved to make my way back to the table.

"Posso offrirti da bere?" he said.

I thought he'd asked me about my drink, so I responded, "It's Chardonnay."

"You speak English?" he asked.

"Yes."

"I offered to buy you a drink. But I see you have one already," he said.

"Yes, thank you anyway."

"Can I buy you dessert?"

"That's generous of you, but I think I'll be sharing dessert with my date," I said and pointed to my now empty table. I turned back and a smile spread across his face.

"He's coming back," I said promptly. "He stepped out to make a phone call."

"Oh, I'm sure he will. He would be crazy to leave someone like you."

"I've heard of this Italian charm. It is flattering, but I should go." I began to move away, but he stopped me by placing his hand on my arm.

"I couldn't help but notice the color of your eyes from across the room," he said. "I had to come closer to see if my own eyes weren't deceiving me. But it's true. They are magnificent." Men commented on my eyes often, but now I wondered if his compliment had greater implications.

"What do you mean?" I asked.

"Only that I've searched for you my whole life," he said.

Right. He's only spewing a line, nothing more.

"Um, thanks," I said and physically lifted his hand off my arm.

"Will you be in town long?" he asked, and before I could answer, another voice responded.

"Is there a problem here?" asked Hunter. His voice resonated deeper than usual. He sounded intense but not necessarily angry.

"No, there's no problem," I said and grabbed Hunter's hand to lead him back to the table. Hunter turned his head and continued to stare at the man.

"What did he want?" asked Hunter, still not making eye contact with me.

"He just wanted to buy me a drink," I said.

"I was barely gone five minutes and the hyenas are already prowling," he spat out.

I frowned at him, confused and a little annoyed at being compared to some fresh meat in the Serengeti.

"That's not what happened. Let's not make this a big deal. I handled it," I said, but I noticed his breathing had quickened and his chest rose rapidly. He still didn't look at me, and I started to worry about the guy at the bar.

"What was your phone call about?" I asked to distract Hunter.

He was not paying attention to me and narrowed his focus at the bar. I placed my hand on his cheek and redirected his focus to my face.

"Your date is right here, not at the bar, unless something else is tempting you there," I said.

Hunter finally shifted his gaze to look at me. He took two large breaths, and I felt the pulse in his neck slowing down.

"That's better," I said. "Now tell me, what did Thomas have to say?"

"He said my father is not improving. Actually, he thinks he's getting worse and that we need to hurry."

"Okay," I said, "Then let's get back to the apartment and get ready for an early morning start."

I stood up and waited for Hunter to reach me as I walked toward the exit. I noticed he caught the eye of the man at the bar again. For a moment, the man no longer looked charming but ready to challenge Hunter. It reminded me of two fighters before a boxing match staring each other down. I didn't think either would give in, so I played coach and pulled Hunter back. "Come on, let's get out of here," I said.

He didn't respond. He gave one last look over his shoulder to the guy at the bar and I couldn't help but hold my breath until I finally dragged Hunter outside.

Eighteen

Michaela

I don't see any street signs, but the driver was certain this was the place," said Hunter.

"Of course he was. He just wanted us out quickly to pick up his next victims," I grumbled. There was something seriously wrong with the drivers in this town.

We walked up to a little stucco cottage and knocked on the door. An older woman, probably in her seventies, answered.

"Si?"

"Sto cercando la signora Tassone," said Hunter, looking for Mrs. Tassone.

The woman pointed to a house up the road and then closed her door.

"So much for Southern hospitality," I said.

This next house was only a tiny bit bigger than the last. It was also made of stone and had a red slate roof. Hunter knocked again. This time a pretty young woman answered the door. She had long black hair, the same length as mine, but hers was straight. I played with the knots in my hair, wishing I had taken more time this morning with it.

"La signora Tassone vive qui?" Hunter inquired if Mrs. Tassone lived there.

"Chi lo vuole sapere?" asked the woman. I stepped forward.

"Tell her Michaela Morrone, Lucia Shedley's daughter, wants to know."

The woman turned to look at me. She appeared to be my age, but somehow, she intimidated me. I stood my ground in this staring contest.

"You are Lucia Shedley's daughter?" she asked, her hand on her cocked hip.

"Oh good, you speak English," I said, relieved I wouldn't have to use my translator app for this conversation. "Yes, I'm her daughter and we are looking for Anna Maria Tassone."

The woman's cool demeanor did not change.

"Lucia Shedley didn't have a daughter. And there is no one who lives here by that name. Good day," she was about to close the door when Hunter put his hand on it to stop her.

"Wait, please," he said patiently while I reeled from her statement. What did she mean Lucia did not have a daughter?

"We've come such a long way. Can you hear us out?" he asked.

"I do not have time to listen to lies. I don't know who you people are, but you need to leave now."

"Why do you think Lucia didn't have a daughter?" I asked.

"Because she never mentioned her."

"You met my mother?" I asked with mixed feelings, happy to bring up my mother's memory again and upset she'd never mentioned me.

"Yes, and you need to leave now."

I pulled off my sunglasses to wipe beneath my eye before any tears could escape. When I looked up, the woman stared into my eyes and hers grew bigger than I ever thought possible.

"Oh, mio Dio!" she gasped. She grabbed my sleeve and pulled me and Hunter into the house and slammed the door behind us.

She pulled open the drapes and turned her head violently from side to side, peering out the window. I had no idea what had just happened, but Hunter did.

"You saw Michaela's eyes. You know we're telling you the truth. Why are you panicking?"

"Did anyone see you knocking?" she asked.

"No, we just arrived here," I said. "Oh wait, Hunter asked the lady down the street if she knew where Anna Maria Tassone lives."

"*Mannaggia,*" she muttered under her breath. "Signora Vincenza never minds her own business. The whole village will know you are looking for my grandmother."

"Anna Maria Tassone is your grandmother?" asked Hunter. "Does she live here with you?"

"I live with her, and she won't let me forget it," she said with a smile. "Even though I could live anywhere else but choose to take care of her, she says I wouldn't want to be anywhere else. And she's right, of course."

"We need to speak with her. Is she here now?" asked Hunter.

"No, she went to the market to pick up some things. She will be back shortly. I am Veronica Tassone." The woman stuck out her hand to Hunter and then to me. She had quite the grip. And just like that, I was intimidated again.

"I'm Hunter Durand. We just need to ask your grandmother a few questions."

She narrowed her eyes at him and then responded, "What sort of questions do you need to ask her?"

"We will get to those when she returns. Can you tell us why you panicked earlier?"

"Some men came knocking on our door years ago. They were looking for Lucia and her husband, Marco. I told them they had left but they didn't believe me. They pushed me aside and rummaged through the whole house. They didn't find anything, of course, and then they harassed my grandmother.

"They asked her where Lucia had gone and if she would be back. But my grandmother said she did not know."

Veronica splayed her hands in front of her as she told the story.

"The next day, we heard that Lucia and Marco's small plane had crashed and fallen into the sea. I asked my grandmother if those men had anything to do with it, but she hushed me. She said we were never to speak of Lucia and Marco again. She said they were now dead and gone. I don't know how she will take the news of you. She was very distraught over their deaths."

The front door opened, and an older woman walked through the entrance. I kept my eyes down, not wanting to shock her.

"Oh, Veronica, hai degli amici?" I believe she asked if we were Veronica's friends.

"Si, nonna. Sono nostri amici," said Veronica, indicating that we were her grandmother's friends, as well.

"Ah, si? Chi sono?" She inquired who we were. I took a deep breath and hoped this woman could handle the news.

"Sono Americani, quindi parliamo inglese," said Veronica, suggesting they speak in English since their guests were American.

"Okay," said the grandmother.

"My grandmother taught me English, so she is quite fluent, as well. She learned it from your mother I believe," Veronica said.

"Your mother?" asked Signora Tassone, sounding a bit confused.

"Yes, nonna, her mother. Please, take a seat. I have some news."

A rustling of footsteps came first, then an older woman appeared just in front of where we stood in the kitchen. She could not have been taller than five feet with a plump body. Her silver hair was cut short, and she wore no makeup.

"Nonna, I know you asked me never to say the name again, but there's something I need to tell you." Veronica took a deep breath then continued, "Nonna, this is Michaela Morrone. Lucia Shedley's daughter."

"No, *non è possibile*. It's not possible," the older woman said stubbornly. "Lucia would have told me if she had a daughter."

I felt this was the right time to reveal myself, and so I turned toward Signora Tassone and stared straight into her eyes.

"*Dio Santo*," she whispered and put her hand over her mouth as tears pooled in her eyes.

"You look just like her when she was your age," she said.

"Signora Tassone, I'm sorry if this comes as a shock to you. I understand my mother never told you about me," I said.

"No, she never told me she had a daughter, but I think I can understand why. Did she mention me? Is that how you found me?" asked Signora Tassone.

"No, she never mentioned you either." I felt like apologizing because I understood the pain those words caused someone who deeply loved my mother.

"We found a letter you sent to her back in March of '08. You asked her to come to the village immediately and to bring her tools. What did you mean by that?" I asked.

"Oh *bella*, this is a long story. We will need fortitude for it. I'll start on dinner and we can discuss this properly over some pasta."

Nineteen

Hunter

The meal was delicious. Signora Tassone made a sauce using tomatoes from her own garden. She fried some zucchini flowers and served them with her homemade wine. It was the best meal I'd had in ages.

I'd been quiet, as I wanted to give Michaela and Signora Tassone time to adjust to the news of each other's existence. The story of Michaela's parents took precedence right now, and she needed to know what had happened to them first. But I had to grind my teeth to refrain from asking Signora Tassone: What could I do to save my father?

As impatient as I felt, for the first time in my life, I wanted to put someone else's needs before my own. I didn't exaggerate when I told Michaela I had fallen. I was in love with her. In all my future plans, I'd envisioned many obstacles, but I never saw her coming.

I would do anything to be with Michaela. I would renounce my kingdom for her if it meant she could truly be mine. That thought scared me a little as the truth of it hit me squarely in the chest. I was willing to lose everything I'd ever known for the chance of a life I'd never imagined. A life away from the Manticore Kingdom.

The sound of dishes rattling snapped my attention back to the room. Veronica sat at the table, having set down a tray with coffee in front of us. I refocused on the conversation, as Signora Tassone said she was ready to tell her story.

"Your grandmother Ramona was my best friend in the village," Signora Tassone began. "We climbed trees on our way back from school, we skipped rocks by the pond, or if the day was hot, we would jump into the pond with our school clothes still on. We were wild in those days. Your grandmother was a social butterfly. She easily charmed anyone she spoke to, and so we got away with a lot."

"That's not how Aunt Julie described her," said Michaela. "She said her mother was more of a recluse."

"Well, she changed after some visitors came to our village. We knew they were not from any neighboring villages because they spoke a different language when they thought no one was around. Ramona and I overheard them one afternoon when we were sitting up in one of the fig trees near her home. I realized after meeting Lucia that the language they were speaking was English, but we were from a tiny village and had never heard those words before.

"They also smoked a different brand of cigarettes, something we had never smelled in our village, and I have not smelled since..."

"Since?" asked Michaela.

"I am getting ahead of myself," continued Signora Tassone. "One day, Ramona told me she must go straight home from school. She could not stop to play, as her mother said there would be visitors for her when she returned that afternoon.

"I teased her that perhaps the next time I saw her, she would be engaged to one of the foreigners. While we were still rambunctious girls, we were thirteen and it was not unheard of for a girl our age to be promised for marriage. Many girls were married at sixteen, and in fact if you were unmarried by twenty, you were considered out of bloom."

Michaela shook her head, but she did not interrupt Signora Tassone again.

"The next morning, I already saw a difference in Ramona. She was pensive and didn't talk much on our walk to school. I asked her what had happened, and she said I was right, that she was engaged to be married to one of the foreigners.

"I was happy for her—most of us wanted to be married as it meant more freedom, but your grandmother did not seem happy. I asked her if her parents had given her a choice in the matter, and she nodded yes but I could see tears forming in her eyes, so I did not press her any further. I did ask her when she would be married, and she said not until she turned sixteen, so she had plenty of time until then. That seemed to console her a bit and we went about our day.

"The foreigners left the next day but over the next two years they would return perhaps three or four times a year. After each visit, Ramona would be quiet again. She would not be herself, and I wished there were something I could do about it. I asked her if she could just call off the engagement and she said it was impossible. During these last two years, I noticed Ramona had grown closer to a boy from our village. His name was Antonio and sometimes he would accompany us on our walks to and from school. It was obvious he, too, was enamored of Ramona—it was hard not to be. She had the same exquisite violet eyes as you, beautiful brown curly hair and curves that made all of us jealous. All my life I found myself a bit envious of Ramona, until she was engaged. Seeing her so upset, I just wanted to take her pain away."

Veronica passed her grandmother a glass of water. Signora Tassone smiled and took a sip.

"About a week before her sixteenth birthday, and two weeks before her fiancé was to arrive for the wedding, I pleaded with Ramona to reconsider. I told her I would help her any way that I could and begged her to call it off.

"Ramona stared at me for a while. She finally said, 'I will be okay, I promise you, Anna Maria. You are my best friend, and no matter what happens, we will always be in each other's hearts. I will never forget you.'

"I was startled, I knew she was getting married, but I had not thought about her leaving the village. Of course, her fiancé would want to bring her back to his home, but as a young woman I had not considered losing my friend so quickly. I hugged her tightly and stroked her hair, telling her over and over that I would miss her and please write to me. She nodded but did not say anything else.

"The next morning, I waited at our usual meeting place, underneath the apple tree, but Ramona never came. I waited perhaps fifteen minutes before I walked to her house and knocked on her door. Signora Shedley answered and looked confused to see me. I asked if Ramona was feeling okay and if she was coming to school. Signora Shedley shook her head and said she didn't understand. Ramona had left her a note on the kitchen table explaining she'd had to leave early to help me with my chores before heading to school. I didn't know how to respond but she didn't wait for a reply. She ran to Ramona's room and stopped when she opened her door. I followed behind her and saw over her shoulder that Ramona's bed was neatly made and there weren't any clothes laying around, but her closet door was open and many of her dresses and hats were missing. Signora Shedley's eyes grew large, and she said, 'What has she done?'

"I didn't know what to do so I quietly left the house. I worried, where could Ramona have gone on her own? Was she safe? Would she be okay? Later that evening, my mother told me that Antonio was also missing, and the entire village concluded that Ramona and Antonio had run off together. It was a scandal people talked about for years. I never heard from Ramona. I never knew what happened to her. I prayed every night for her, but I never knew for sure that she was all right until I heard from your mother."

"My mother?" asked Michaela.

"Yes, one day I found your mother at my doorstep, much like Veronica found you today," she said with a hint of a smile. "I was transported to that day more than twenty years ago when this beautiful woman told me she was Ramona Shedley's daughter. I cried tears of joy when I heard that name, and that Ramona was alive and had a daughter. Your mother and I talked for hours.

"Lucia told me how she'd found a box filled with letters addressed to me that her mother had written. My friend Ramona had written to me every day for a year, then every week and then every few months for years, but she'd never mailed any of them. She had placed them in envelopes and written down my address on each one but maybe was too afraid that the letters would be traced, and she would be found.

"I asked Lucia how she'd convinced her mother to let her visit, but she said she hadn't told her mother she was here. She had graduated high school, and her mother knew she was travelling in Europe, but Lucia kept her visit to our village a secret. She wanted to find the man who wanted to marry her mother."

Michaela raised her eyebrow at this. "Why would my mother want to do that?"

"She said the man knew things no one else did. He was some sort of teacher or expert or something. Lucia said she was old enough to make her own decisions and wanted to find him to ask him some questions."

Signora Tassone paused and wrung her hands on her lap.

"I did not know what to do. I was certain Signora Shedley would know how to get in contact with Ramona's old fiancé. But I felt like I was betraying my friend if I helped her daughter find this man. But I also knew how much Ramona's mother had grieved the loss of her daughter all these years. It would give the old woman peace to know her daughter had not only lived but she had a granddaughter. I could not live with myself if I did not give Signora Shedley the opportunity to meet her granddaughter. So, I agreed to take her there and introduce her.

"I think I was more nervous than your mother walking up to Signora Shedley's door. I knocked once and waited. Your mother stood proud and ready. When the door opened and Signora Shedley saw who was on the other side, she recognized her right away. She later told me it felt as though her heart had travelled the world and returned home at last. She embraced Lucia and told her to come in. I excused myself, as I did not want to intrude on their reunion. And if I am honest, I felt a little guilty that I had done all this behind Ramona's back. So, I left.

"The next day, Lucia came to visit me, and she told me they had contacted the fiancé last night and he would be coming to the village any day now. She seemed so excited by the prospect; I couldn't help comparing her reaction to her mother's. They looked the same but were not similar. Your mother looked ready to take on the world and not run away from anyone or anything."

I leaned forward and squeezed Michaela's hand. She squeezed back.

"The man arrived only two days later. I saw him walking in the village market with Lucia one day. Even though more than twenty years had passed, I recognized him right away. I also smelled the distinct aroma of his cigarettes when he walked by. Lucia looked happy, hanging on to every word he said. He stayed for nearly a month that summer. It would not be the last time that I saw him, however. Each summer, your mother would meet him here for a few weeks.

"I asked your mother, one year, if she was still hiding these summer visits from her mother. She said she wasn't. She told me that she was proud of the work she did and had told her mother everything. Ramona did not take the news well. She was angry with her daughter for going back to her village and meeting with that man. I asked Lucia if I could have her mother's address so I could write to her and explain my role in this. But Lucia said she did not know where her mother was. She had left shortly after they'd argued and hadn't contacted her since."

Michaela sucked in a breath. "I always thought my grandmother was dead," she said. "My mother just said she was gone so I assumed she'd died. Oh my God, could she still be alive?"

The anguish in Michaela's voice pushed me off my seat. But before I could comfort her, Signora Tassone had Michaela in her arms.

"Hush, *bella*. If your grandmother is still alive, she does not want to be found. I've learned that lesson many times over the years," Signora Tassone said quietly to Michaela.

Michaela nodded and wiped away her tears. I wished I could do that for her, but Signora Tassone had it under control.

"Why didn't my mother tell me any of this?" asked Michaela.

"I don't know. Lucia did tell me she hated how her mother had made decisions for her. Lucia said she would never do that to her own daughter. But in the last few years, she was not happy. Perhaps it was the work she did. Perhaps she wanted to keep you away from it," said Signora Tassone.

"That's what I don't understand. What was she learning? What sort of answers was she seeking?"

"I wish I knew," said Signora Tassone. "I feel responsible, as I was the one who called her over here when she came back in March. Signora Shedley had passed earlier in January, and the man knew I was the only one who still kept in contact with Lucia. So, he asked me to write to your mother, tell her she needed to come immediately and to bring her tools. I didn't know what it meant, but he was a very serious man. I did not argue. I regret that letter every day," said Signora Tassone.

"They said my parents' plane crashed over the Adriatic Sea. They said it was an accident," said Michaela but she paused before she could finish.

She seemed to struggle to ask the question she both wanted and feared to know.

"Do you think it was an accident, Signora Tassone?"

"I don't know, *bella*," she said. "I ask myself this question every day."

Signora Tassone's eyebrows creased, and she held her forehead with her hand, her elbow on the table.

"When your mother and father came in March of '08 they did not seem happy. I asked your mother what was going on and she said she was done. She said she no longer wanted to be a part of this anymore. I asked her what she meant, but she told me the less I knew the better. The next day, I read in the paper that a small plane with three passengers crashed, and Lucia and Marco were in it. The paper named your mother and father, but I did not recognize the name of the pilot. Was it an accident or did someone mean for her to die on that plane? I don't know if we'll ever know."

"How do I get ahold of my mother's mentor?" I asked.

"I'm not sure, only Signora Shedley knew how to contact him. He called me after Signora Shedley died and asked me to write to Lucia, but I never knew how to reach him."

Michaela rubbed her hands on her knees. She had hoped to get answers today, but all we had were more questions, more unknowns. And I still didn't know how Michaela or her family could help save my father.

I rose from my chair to stand next to the window and released a frustrated breath. We had nothing concrete to move forward with. This trip was just another dead end. I felt we were close to uncovering something but were still missing important pieces to solving this puzzle.

My phone buzzed in my pocket. It was Thomas.

"Thomas, is everything all right?"

"Hunter. I'm afraid your father is worse. His heartbeat is barely there, and his breathing is labored now. The physician has not been able to get an antidote together. Have you discovered anything?"

"We are searching, Thomas, but nothing is clear yet."

"In that case, I think you should return. I don't know how much longer he will live, and I know you would want to be here should things take a turn for the worst."

I shut my eyes, not wanting to believe that all hope was lost. I was so sure we could find a way to save him. I was so sure the path was through Michaela. I stared at her beautiful face. Her eyes shimmered with pain; she, too, dealt with family heartache. She had not received the answers she'd come here for either.

We did know, however, that there was more to Michaela and her family than she had imagined. Her mother was a part of something her grandmother had run from—twice. And maybe in the end it had even killed Lucia. Signora Tassone knew nothing more. It was time to move on from this place. I needed to be with my father.

"Signora Tassone. Thank you for your hospitality, but we need to get back. My father is not well." I met Michaela's eyes, and knew when she nodded that she understood the situation back home had become grave.

"I will leave you with my card. Should this man ever try to get in contact with you again, please tell him to call this number."

"I will. And be careful, both of you."

Twenty

Michaela

The taxi driver who drove us back to the airport was the complete opposite of the one who'd picked us up. This guy was in no rush and was on his third story about his childhood friend. I would have found it endearing if I weren't so exhausted. I didn't know what time it was, but my body definitely hadn't adjusted to the time change. That was probably a good thing since we were heading back home. I frowned and rested my head on Hunter's shoulder. Home. That was two different places for us. The thought made me sad. I wasn't ready for us to be apart.

"Hunter, I don't want to go back to Toronto yet. I would like to meet your father. I know he's not well but if he only has a few days left, I want to be there. I want to be that person you can turn to for support."

"Michaela, my life is complicated. It's not as simple as bringing my girlfriend home to meet my dad," he explained.

I smiled despite the gravity of the situation. "Did you just call me your girlfriend?"

My head still lay on his shoulder, so I couldn't see his face. But his voice told me that he was smiling too. "Yes, I did."

"I like the sound of that."

"I do too. But, as much as I want you there, I can't expose...I can't expose you to my family just yet."

I was a little hurt that he didn't want me to be there, but I didn't know what else to say. It drove me crazy that he was keeping secrets from me. Then, I wondered, had I just become another secret he would keep?

Whether it was his hesitation to introduce me to his family or the emotions from the last few days finally bursting through, tears fell down my face and I couldn't stop them. I held my breath and tried not to make a sound. I didn't want him to hear me cry. I was stronger than this. I blamed the jet lag.

"Hey, hey, are you crying?" Hunter asked gently as he tried to lift my head from his shoulder.

"No," I said and wiped the tears from my eyes.

"Oh, Michaela. Don't you know how much I care for you? Don't you know that if I could shout it from the rooftops, I'd tell not just my family but the whole world that you are mine?"

He tilted my head so I could look at him. He continued, "I promise this isn't like the last time. I am not saying goodbye. I just need time to deal with what's happening at home right now, and then we will find a way to be together. I will find a way, Michaela. I promise you that." He turned his body so he could face me and said, "Because, sweetheart, I can't breathe without you. My heart stops when you're near but it can't beat without you. I feel it every time I kiss you, I feel it right here."

He took my hand and placed it on his chest. He then stole a kiss from my lips and kept taking until there was no breath left in me. His tongue explored my mouth, and I felt lightheaded as I tried to take a breath. I moved my head back to gasp for air when he said, "Is that too much?"

"No." I shook my head. "It's not enough." And I kissed him back just as deeply.

"*Scusatemi, siamo arrivati.*" The driver interrupted us to tell us we'd arrived.

I sighed and hoped to continue this soon.

Hunter didn't get out of the car; he remained inside with his eyes closed.

"I'm trying to get my breathing under control," he said.

I smiled and told him I'd get the bags. But he was up and helping before I even got one out of the trunk.

I looked around for our airline entrance but couldn't find it.

"Excuse me, sir, but where is Air Canada?"

Hunter translated what I'd said to the driver, and he motioned to an area around the building.

"Well, a little closer would have been nice," I mumbled. I really needed to get some sleep and some coffee.

Thank goodness I'd splurged on more expensive luggage—the kind with four wheels instead of two—when I bought it years ago for my first vacation to the Dominican Republic. Ah, that had been a great trip. I thought Hunter and I should go to the Dominican together, once all this crazy stuff was under control.

Hunter had paid the driver and caught up to me when I turned to him to say, "I don't see the Air Canada gate. I don't see any gates on this side."

Hunter looked around and then went still.

"Michaela, get down!" he shouted and used his body to cover mine as shots fired above us.

Oh my God, what just happened?

Hunter popped his head up to look around the building.

"Quickly, we need to move," he said and helped me to my feet.

The shots caused several officers to race outside with their guns drawn. Hunter pointed the officers in the direction the shots had been fired.

"I didn't see the shooter, but the bullets came from there." He pointed to the left of the building, near the highway.

An officer ushered us inside and asked for our passports. He brought us to a small room and told us to sit. He ran background checks, I assumed, to see if we were fugitives or something. We waited thirty minutes alone in the room. When the man came back, he asked us where we were headed. Hunter told him New York. He took a statement from us and said he would be in touch if he needed anything further. Then he let us go.

When I tried to stand, I shook from my head down to my toes. I didn't know if the chill came from the cool air inside the airport or the trauma of being shot at and questioned. I sat down again at the nearest bench outside the office.

"I'll get you some water. Will you be all right if I leave you here for a minute?" asked Hunter. "I'll be right over there. I'll have my eye on you the whole time."

He pointed to a kiosk, and I nodded because I didn't know if I could speak yet. I hadn't said much since the shots rang out.

As my racing thoughts slowed down, I tried to process what had happened. Someone had tried to shoot us. Someone had tried to kill me.

Oh my God, what have I done?

What have I gotten myself into?

Tremors wracked my body and my teeth chattered. I spied Hunter paying for our waters and snacks. He caught my eye and must have realized I was spiraling because he rushed over.

He put the water and food down and held me up.

"I'm here for you. You're all right. You're not hurt. You are going to be fine. Do you hear me? Everything is going to be fine, Michaela."

He kept repeating these words while stroking my hair, my cheek, my arms. I felt him everywhere, but I was still cold. I squeezed his ribs and held on tight, never wanting to let go.

"Someone tried to kill me," I said softly into his shirt.

"I'm going to kill them," he whispered.

I probably wouldn't have heard him if his mouth wasn't so close to my ear. I felt the rage inside those words, and my body shivered.

Hunter sat down next to me and put one arm around me as he used his other hand to grab his phone.

"I need to make a call. It will just be a minute."

I nodded, not caring who he called as long as he continued to hold me.

"Thomas, I need you to change an airline ticket for me and email it to me ASAP. I need you to change Michaela's flight from Toronto to New York. Yes, that's right. Immediately."

He ended the call and covered my hand with his.

"I guess I'm going to New York?" I should have been happy about this news, but I only felt numb.

"Yes. I'm not letting you out of my sight. Someone tried to hurt you and I'm not about to let that happen. I won't let anyone hurt you. Ever. I promise. I will protect you with my own life."

The steel in his voice could have cut a rock. I feared it but revelled in its fierceness at the same time. I had always considered myself a strong woman, but I wasn't ashamed to say I was crumbling right now and needed support.

Knowing he was next to me, I stood up and took the next step. My legs were a little sturdier and my breathing was normal again. I hoped we could outrun whoever was trying to catch us.

Twenty-One

Michaela

We'd arrived in New York but weren't heading to Hunter's apartment. He drove us to his father's home instead. It was dark outside but the homes in this neighborhood lit up the streets like it was Christmas time.

There were pot lights underneath eavestroughs, floodlights shining on trees, and even spotlights on rocks to showcase the house numbers. The lighting completely transformed the landscape. It wasn't just the ambience that was impressive. The houses were at least three times bigger than my family home, and many had gates surrounding the property.

I turned to watch Hunter. I couldn't see his eyes. He wasn't looking at me but stared at the road ahead. Tension radiated off of him as we wound through the neighborhood. His knuckles were white from his grip on the steering wheel.

He pulled up to the largest mansion I'd ever seen. The stonework on the house reminded me of homes from the nineteenth century—until Hunter drove up to one of the four garages along the side and used an automatic door opener. That brought me back to the present day. Hunter parked the rental car inside and I slowly got out. My heart raced and a bead of sweat formed at my hairline.

He held my hand as we entered his father's home together. I barely had a moment to bask in the glory of walking into my boyfriend's family home hand-in-hand when a man entered the foyer and asked, "What is she doing here?"

The man had dark hair like Hunter's, only it was much longer than his. There was a family resemblance, and I recognized him as one of the men Hunter had dined with at Savor. That night seemed so long ago now.

"John. This is none of your concern," said Hunter.

"I beg to differ, cousin. You have brought a stranger into the family home at a private time."

"She is not a stranger. She is my girlfriend," said Hunter sternly. I was just as annoyed as Hunter. I didn't understand why John would care one way or the other. It was his uncle's home, not his.

"She's your what?" he asked, his voice rising.

Geesh, I was a pretty good prize, thank you very much. No need to sound surprised.

From the corner of my eye, I spotted Leo walking toward the foyer from a darkened hallway. Did these people all live here or something?

"You heard me, John." And to his other cousin, Hunter said, "Leo, I'm glad you're here. Michaela and I will go see my father first, but we need to have a family meeting. Can you gather everyone to meet in the dining room in thirty minutes?"

"Hello, Michaela. It's nice to see you again," Leo said with a smile. Then he straightened his mouth and addressed Hunter, "My father is not back from Europe yet."

"When is Davis expected to return?"

"In a couple of weeks," replied Leo.

"All right. Gather everyone else. I'll be there shortly."

Leo had a strange look about him; his forehead slightly creased, as though he was trying to assess the situation.

So am I, Leo. So am I.

I smiled at him and offered him a nod, unsure of what to say in this situation.

Hunter grabbed my hand and led me up the carpeted staircase. Dark wood paneling lined the sides of the staircase, which continued up into the upstairs foyer. The foyer was grand with a cathedral ceiling above and marble statues poised along the walls. The statues looked like they were centuries old.

Goodness, could they be authentic? If they really were genuine, they should lock these pieces up.

There was a room at the end of the hallway with a light streaming through its open door. Inside, an older man lay in his bed, I assumed this was Hunter's father. What looked to be a physician stood beside him, listening to the patient's heart with a stethoscope.

"Oh, Hunter, you're back. That's good," said the man.

"How is he?" asked Hunter.

"There's been no improvement, I'm afraid. In fact, his breathing sounds worse, but at least his heart is steady," he explained.

"And the antidote?"

"Unfortunately, I've come across a number of stumbling blocks. Whenever I think I'm close to creating the perfect counter dose, the chemical does not react the way I expect it to. I've never run into anything like this before, but I'm not going to give up."

"No, and neither am I," said Hunter. "He is going to make it through this." Hunter's voice held conviction, and if his voice could heal his father, the strength of it would.

"Can you give us a minute alone with him?" asked Hunter.

"Yes, of course. I will be downstairs if you need me," said the physician before he left the room.

I hovered near the edge of the bed, wanting to give Hunter some space. He pulled two chairs from a nearby table and brought them up to his father's bedside. He gestured for me to sit next to him. I did.

"Father, I want you to meet Michaela," he said. "You would probably flirt with her if you were feeling better," he said with a smile. "She is special. She's not who I expected to come into my life and probably not what you expected either."

He grabbed his father's hand and then mine. "But I want to make this work. I want your blessing and hope to have it when you are well again. I'd hoped Michaela and her family could heal you, but we haven't figured that out yet."

He released his father's hand but still held mine. "But, there is still hope. As you've always said, if there's breath in these lungs and a beat to my heart then I have all the strength that I need in my soul."

Hunter stopped and squeezed my hand while looking at his father. "I know you will pull through. I know you will." He made a fist with his free hand and placed it on his father's chest. "I need you to get better and help me. Help me find a way to build a life with the woman I love."

I was stunned by his words, the intimacy of them, the honesty and fierceness behind them. I squeezed his hand and turned to him to say, "I love you too, Hunter," and then gave him a quick kiss on his cheek.

We sat in silence for a few minutes before Hunter glanced down at his watch.

"I have to go. The family is waiting for me downstairs. Will you be all right here?"

"Yes, I'll be fine. Go, and good luck," I said.

He kissed my lips this time, and I brought my hand to his neck. I felt his heartbeat quicken underneath my palm. "I love you," he said again.

I smiled and whispered, "Love you too."

With a final look back at me and his father, Hunter left the room.

I sat there, uncertain of what I should say or do. I reached out to hold the man's hand. It felt cold and heavy. I touched the roughness of his fingertips and the tendons that ran down his knuckles. They felt like powerful hands. His fingers were long, and I felt a slight sensation in his veins when I put my fingers on top of them. I bowed my head and did the only thing I could do. I prayed. I prayed for his health to return. I prayed for whatever ailed him to leave his body. I prayed that I would have the chance to meet this man Hunter loved so much. Words my mother taught me started to fall from my lips. I closed my eyes and allowed my senses to take over.

Twenty-Two

Hunter

I took a moment to acknowledge everyone sitting at the table with a nod. My sister Laura, my aunt Elenora, her son Leo, Aunt Olympia, Uncle Theodore, and his son John. They were all important members of this family and now would be jurors to my private life.

I didn't like having to justify my relationship to others, but in this case, it couldn't be left unsaid. I had to put it all on the table, and then I would leave it in this room for good. That was my plan.

"Thank you all for meeting me here. I know it is short notice." Everyone in the room remained silent—I had their undivided attention.

"I'm not sure how much you've heard, so I will start from the beginning. I met a woman named Michaela a few weeks ago here in New York, but I first saw her at one of Laura's parties."

"A human girl," John said.

I glared at him for interrupting me. He looked down and fidgeted with one of his rings but didn't look sufficiently intimidated in my opinion.

"Yes, I am getting to that, John. Michaela is human. Early on, I tried to end the relationship, as I know the rules. There can be no intimate relationships with humans, and certainly not marriage. As difficult as it was, I let her go."

Laura comforted me with sympathetic eyes. She'd seen the intensity of my feelings for Michaela that first night. She knew how difficult it was for me then. But it wasn't Laura I was here to convince. So, I went on.

"So, what happened?" asked Uncle Theodore. "What changed?"

"When Aunt Olympia said our only hope was to find the one with the violet eyes, I had no choice but to seek her out again," I explained.

Aunt Olympia gasped at the other end of the table.

"You found her? You found the one with the violet eyes?" A new hope glimmered in her eyes. I hated that I had to snuff it out.

"Yes, she's here. But she doesn't know anything about her abilities. We are not even certain she has any," I said.

"But that doesn't mean it isn't possible, Hunter," she said, hope still alive and well on her face. "Perhaps we can take her to meet our professors—maybe one of them will know what she is."

"What she is, is human," said John. "We cannot have a human parading around our kingdom, meeting our professors, knowing our secrets. This is absurd. Listen, I know we all want Marsel to live, but we cannot risk all the manticores' secrets for it."

"It is King Marsel, and we are not risking anything," I ground out. "Michaela does not know what we are, but she may suspect we are more than just human. I agree, it's not a good idea to expose her to any other manticores outside of our family, including those in this house. The staff must not know what she is, whether it is human or something more."

I looked each of them in the eye when I said this last part. Satisfied, I went on.

"We found a trunkful of tomes in Michaela's family home. They may be the key to uncovering more truths. I brought one of these tomes back with me. I will head over to the kingdom tomorrow and seek out a professor I can trust to review it. We shall see if one of the professors knows where we could discover more. I still believe she is the key to saving our king, and we must try everything in our power to do so." I pounded the table with my fist. I couldn't help the anguish I felt for not having found a way to save my father. *Dammit!* I would not give up, and neither could those around me.

"Is this about saving the king or saving your heart, Hunter?" asked Aunt Elenora.

I took a deep breath before I responded. "I do not deny I care deeply for Michaela. I do not deny that I won't stop until I find a way for us to be together and that she will be a part of my life. However, right now, she is also our only hope to save the king."

"How can you be together? She is not a manticore. She cannot know our secrets," Aunt Elenora pressed me again.

"I don't know how, but I do know that I will find a way. I will uphold the law, but I will not give her up for anyone or anything."

"Will you renounce your right to the throne for her?" asked Aunt Elenora. "You cannot be king with a human wife. She cannot produce a manticore heir."

"While there is still breath in the king's body and his heart still beats, there will be no more talk of another king. Do I make myself clear?"

"Crystal, nephew," said Aunt Elenora with a Cheshire cat smile.

"Then we are clear," I began, but before I could finish that sentence, Thomas ran into the room.

"Hunter, you must come now," said Thomas.

"Why? What has happened?" I asked.

"It's the king. He is trying to speak," he said.

"Father is awake?" I asked, not believing my own words.

"No, not quite awake, but...Hurry you must see for yourself," he said and held the door open for me. I didn't need any further prompting. I rushed out of my chair to see what had happened.

When I arrived inside my father's bedroom, I faced a familiar scene. The physician leaned over him, listening to his heart with a stethoscope; except this time, Michaela was also there by my father's side, holding his hand. The tableau stopped me in my tracks. Her beauty always arrested me, but now the compassion on her face nearly brought me to my knees.

"Hunter," she said, with a brilliant smile on her face. The physician called my name and I pulled myself away from her gaze.

"Hunter. Good you're here," he said.

"What's happened?" I asked.

"Well, there's been a change—perhaps even a slight improvement. When I came in to check on him, his breathing was less labored, nearly smooth. He seems to be breathing deeply and soundly now," he explained.

"Thomas mentioned something about speaking," I said, hoping to confirm if this was true.

"Well, not speaking exactly, but he moved his lips earlier. It looked as though he was trying to say something. I needed to calm him down. I worried agitation could set him back. Michaela managed to soothe him until he fell back asleep. He appears to be resting peacefully now."

I stared at Michaela, who was still holding my father's hand, rubbing her thumb along the top of it with one hand and running her fingers through his hair with her other.

This woman made me vulnerable. I could lay myself at her feet right now and beg her to find me good enough for her. She held a power over me that scared me to death. Such effortless movements, small caresses, and I was at her mercy.

Could her touch have healed my father? Could it be that simple? I dared not voice my thoughts in front of the doctor. The rest of the family entered the room.

"What's going on?" asked Uncle Theodore.

The physician recounted the same explanation he'd given me moments ago. Uncle Theodore immediately looked at Michaela, who still held my father's hand, then at me. His eyes told me his suspicions mirrored mine. He believed Michaela was responsible for the king's improvement.

Another thought, this time a fear, entered my mind: What if they wanted to use her for their own benefit? Forced her to use her gifts for themselves? I would not let that happen. A growl grew in my chest, but I held it down.

"Was this her doing?" Uncle Theodore finally asked the question we were all thinking.

"Not here" was all I said as I motioned with my head that we should leave the room. Once everyone was outside, I shut the door. The physician, however, was a manticore so I was careful of what I said in case he overheard. "We do not know what caused the king's change. I am cautiously optimistic that it is a change in the right direction and that the king will recover. However, we do not know if Michaela had anything to do with it. It may all just be a coincidence." I stared everyone in the eye to ensure they understood what I'd said.

Aunt Olympia smiled from ear to ear; she obviously felt Michaela had something to do with this.

"I will continue with my plan to bring the book to the professors tomorrow. If there is more to Michaela than we know, I am confident it's in those books. Until we know more, we do not bother Michaela with any of this. She is not aware of her abilities, and frankly we are not even sure she has any, so no further speculation."

Everyone nodded and seemed to agree—for now. However, I knew that in a family bred for power, something like the ability to heal would not be ignored for long.

I returned to the bedroom and walked over to my father's bedside. I heard why the doctor was optimistic. My father's breathing was unlabored, even and, yes, even peaceful. I could now hear his heartbeat, even without a stethoscope.

I held my hand out to Michaela and helped her rise to her feet.

"Thank you," I whispered into her ear.

"For what?" she asked.

"For staying here with him. For holding his hand. For being you," I said.

She smiled and rose on her toes to kiss my cheek. "I would do anything for you, Hunter," she said.

My heart was full of things I would do for her, but this wasn't the place to tell her. I led her away from the room and let the physician know to call me if there were any more changes.

"Do you mind if we stay here tonight?" I asked her. "We can stay in my old room."

"I don't mind. Is there enough room for the two of us?" she asked.

"It's a king bed," I said.

"Oh, just the one?"

I laughed because she was cheeky when she flirted. "Yep, just the one."

I reached and held her face between the palms of my hands and said, "I don't want to be away from you ever again. I will fight to control everything within me to lie next to you and make sure you are safe. Are you all right with that?"

"Mmm, I can make it work," she said. Then she sauntered away, making her grand exit. I waited a few seconds, and then she popped her head back in. "Um, where's your room?"

I laughed because, truly, how could I resist? I grabbed her hand and led her to the other end of the hallway toward my old bedroom.

Twenty-Three

Hunter

Last night was one of the worst and best nights of my life. Lying next to Michaela felt right. But only being able to hold her against me, and nothing more, was utter torture.

I remembered the first time I saw her in Toronto, and then in New York City. I recalled my visceral reaction to her, my instinct to possess her. The instinct was still there, but the more time I spent with Michaela, and the more familiar her scent became, the better I was able to control it. My more typical male instincts were the ones I struggled with now.

I craved her body, but I could not risk losing control and biting her. It was in my nature to playfully nip, but if I were to accidentally break through her skin, the venom that resided in my body would make her ill—or worse, kill her. Even if I could manage to control my bite, it still wouldn't be enough to truly be with her. My seed would surely poison her. I wouldn't give up, though. There was more to Michaela than either of us knew. I was sure of it.

She slept soundly in my arms. I had been watching her sleep since the sun rose about an hour ago. I would willingly watch her sleep every morning for the rest of my life.

I turned toward the nightstand and picked up my phone. It was seven o'clock. I had to get up.

I turned toward the slumbering woman on my arm and placed a kiss on her neck. Her scent stirred my desire. I wouldn't mind a few more minutes holding her in my arms. I stroked her forehead and then her curly hair, which wound across my other arm. My ministrations woke her, but I was in no rush to get out of bed now. With her eyes still closed, I pressed my lips against hers and felt her take in a breath. I sealed her mouth and moved my body to rest on top of hers. I lifted my elbows to protect her body and not crush her with my weight. She moaned, and the sound sent a shiver down my spine.

I moved my lips to her throat and then to her shoulder. She ran her fingers through my hair and pushed me farther down her body. I kissed her breast through the thin T-shirt she wore, the material no match for my determination. But it was a good shield, one that I needed to keep me in check. I held tightly onto my control. I concentrated on every move I made, every flicker of my tongue and every touch of my fingertips on her flesh. When she whispered my name, my body responded in anticipation. I fought harder for control, but my instincts grew stronger until all I wanted was to be inside of her.

With a growl, I flung myself off the bed. The room was silent except for both of us panting.

"What's wrong?" she asked.

When I wrestled my breathing under control, I lied. "Nothing's wrong. I just need to get going. I'll hop in the shower and be back in a few minutes."

She nodded, but her hand lay flat against her heart. I'd bet it was beating as hard as mine was right now.

Thirty minutes later, we were in the dining room sharing an enormous breakfast with my entire family. My family rarely ate all together anymore, but no one wanted to miss a moment of how this all unfolded.

I agreed to update them at dinner this evening if we uncovered anything of importance at the academy today. I had only one book with me. I hoped it would be enough to get us some answers.

Before I left, I dreaded having to tell Michaela I needed to go about this alone.

"Michaela, I don't know how to say this, so I'm just going to say it," I began. She raised her eyebrows at me. I'd got her back up. Not a good way to start.

"I need to take the book from your parents' home to a few professors today," I said.

"I know, we're about to head there now," she said, looking confused.

"Yes, but I need to take them there alone," I clarified.

"You...oh...Why?" she asked the obvious question. The one I didn't know how to answer.

"Because the place I'm going has restricted access. It's not open to the public," I said, trying not to lie, but I had by omission.

She sensed it too.

"Look, I know there are things about your life that you don't think I'll understand. But I love you, Hunter," she said and cupped my cheek. "I will accept whatever it is you're hiding from me."

I nearly revealed my secret then and there. I clamped down on my jaw to hold myself back. Despite her sincerity, I had to maintain the rules.

"It's not that easy, Michaela. I would tell you, only I'm bound not to say a word. I could put many others in jeopardy. I won't do that."

"Fine. I don't get it, but I'll try to be patient. One day, you are going to have to tell me, Hunter."

"One day, I hope I'll have the answers to explain everything to you."

"One day soon," she added and raised her eyebrow again for good measure.

Her tenacity made me smile, and I couldn't help but agree to her demands.

"One day soon," I promised.

She brushed a loose curl behind her ear and fidgeted with the strand.

"Actually, the extra time is good. I need to call my aunt Julie today. I have to tell her everything we learned in Italy—minus the shooting."

After giving Michaela a proper goodbye in the foyer, and promising to be back before dinner, I grabbed the briefcase with the book in it and put it in my car. Michaela was there to see me off, and I took the opportunity to hug and kiss her once more before she headed back inside.

As soon as she closed the door, I dialed Tony's number.

"Hey, Hunter," said Tony.

"Are you in place?" I asked.

"Yes. In the black car behind you. Good view of the front and back of the house," he said.

"Good. Keep your eyes on her at all times. If anyone suspicious approaches the house, you call for backup and you don't let anyone near her. Do you hear me?"

"Absolutely, don't worry. I got this."

"Guard her with your life," I said and ended the call.

Michaela

After Hunter left, I returned to his old bedroom to call my aunt Julie in private. I was nervous about the call, unsure what I would say. I sat in a chair next to the window and dialed her number. She answered immediately.

"Michaela, dear. How are you?" she asked. She sounded pleasant and in a good mood. I hoped I wasn't about to ruin it.

"I'm good, Aunt Julie," I responded.

"How was Italy? Were you able to track down the woman who wrote the letter?"

"Yes. That's why I'm calling you," I said and strummed my fingers on the table. I didn't know where to begin. "Have you been lying to me?" I asked.

"What? What are you talking about?"

"Signora Tassone told me that my grandmother didn't die. That she simply left us. Did you know this?"

There was no response on the other end. I sighed, realizing the truth.

"How could you lie to me?" I demanded.

"Your mother thought it would be easier for you, thinking your grandmother had died rather than abandoning us," Aunt Julie said softly. "I wanted to tell you the truth after your parents died, but then you distanced yourself from me."

"Please, don't blame me," I whispered.

"I'm not blaming you, Michaela. I'm only offering an explanation. I didn't want to burden you further. You already had a lot on your shoulders."

I held back a sob, but a tear escaped. I wiped it away angrily.

"I'm just tired of people keeping things from me for my own good," I said, and an image of Hunter flashed in my mind.

"You're right. We made those decisions with the best intentions, but it was still wrong," she said, and then softly, "I'm sorry."

I held my head in my hand and cried softly.

"I know what it feels like to lose a mother," said Aunt Julie. "Mine may not be dead, but I'm alone all the same."

I sniffled and grabbed a tissue to wipe my nose.

"You're right. It's pretty selfish of me to only think of what I lost," I said.

"You have no idea, Michaela. For so long, I prayed that I would one day run into her at the grocery store or catch a glimpse of her face in a crowded room. But she's gone. I've come to accept it."

"I'm sorry, too," I whispered.

I sucked in a deep breath and held it until my chest burned. Then I slowly let it out.

"Did you know about the fiancé?" I asked.

"Your mother got engaged in Italy?" Aunt Julie asked.

"No, not my mother," I explained. "Yours."

"Really?"

"Get comfortable. This is a long story," I said and curled into a chair myself.

Twenty-Four

Hunter

The drive to Central Park was easier than it had been a couple of weeks ago when Fashion Week was underway. I reached the parking garage above the kingdom and parked in my usual spot. There were more people than usual there that day.

When the elevator reached the ground floor and the doors opened to the narrow hallway, I noticed a group of guards huddling a short distance away. One of them saw me and approached.

"Hunter, I'm glad Leo notified you, but we have everything under control now," he said.

I tried not to act surprised by his statement and nodded once.

"Good. Now, can you recap what happened here?" I asked.

"Well, as I explained to Leo, one of the night guards heard someone walk past while he shut his eyes for a quick rest. He says he wasn't sleeping, just resting. And I believe him, as he quickly followed the suspicious figure," he explained.

I controlled my frustration, as the guard had in fact done his duty despite "resting."

"Go on," I said.

"Well, he followed at a distance so that he could see what the figure was up to. By the time he rounded the second corner, he said that Jenkins's cell was open, and two figures were racing down the hallway.

"He shouted at them to stop, and Jenkins turned to see who it was, but the other one kept running. The guard managed to tackle Jenkins and handcuff him again. But the accomplice got away."

"Is Jenkins locked up once again?" I asked.

"Yes, sir, and we handcuffed him to the wall."

I walked past the group of guards and headed to the dungeons to see for myself. Why didn't Leo tell me any of this?

I reached the predator's cell, where he sat on a dirty cot with one hand indeed cuffed to the wall. His hair was still long and greasy, and he looked even dirtier than before. Despite his dire situation, he had a smile on his face. The smile reminded me of the look he'd had in the courtroom when my father announced his ruling. He was working with someone in the kingdom, and I needed to find out who. It could be the same person who had poisoned my father.

"Who helped you escape?" I demanded.

He said nothing, just kept smiling.

"I saw you smile at someone inside the courtroom. Who was it?" He glanced up at me, a look of appreciation in his eyes. He thought no one had noticed, but I had. He looked down again and said nothing.

"You will be punished for your silence if you do not tell me," I warned.

"Little heir, you are the one who will be punished, not me," he said in a low voice.

"I've committed no crime, whereas you've committed a number of them," I countered.

"Is it a crime to be who I am? To live as nature intended me to live?" he snarled, his voice louder.

"Yes, it is. What you did is against our laws."

"Your laws, not mine. Not everyone sees it as you do. There are many of us who believe we should be the ones ruling this earth," he said and yanked on his chain. A chunk of concrete fell off of the wall. "Our kind is older, stronger, and more worthy than humans. Why should we have to hide who we are?"

"Because what you propose is at best destructive and at worst, it is rape and murder."

"What *you* propose is for us to be some neutered, domesticated pets and we will not take it anymore!" he shouted. This time when he pulled against his chain, I noticed his fingernails had lengthened. He hid his teeth, but I suspected those, too, had sharpened.

"Who helped you?" I said, softer this time. I struggled to keep my own anger and instincts in check.

He laughed and shook his cuffed hand. "I am not the only one who will be chained in this dungeon. Watch your back, little heir—the lion pride is not so loyal."

His words left me reeling. Was the traitor someone I knew? Was the traitor someone in my father's home? Or was this the predator's plan? Did he want me to accuse my family and tear us apart from the inside? I had to review the security footage from my father's home when I returned.

"You will remain cuffed to the wall until you tell us who helped you. My father may have been lenient with you, but I am not my father," I said and leaned in closer. "Pray that he lives. Otherwise, you will deal with me."

I imagined sinking my teeth into his neck and ripping out his heart with my bare hands. "I promise you—I am not some neutered, domesticated pet. Should you disobey me, you will feel my wrath tear your body piece by piece."

This time his smile grew larger. "You're right. You are not like your father. There is hope for you yet."

His words made me regret mine. The animal inside me wanted to pounce and release its anger on the bastard, but he was right. Did that make me more like him and less like my father?

My mind was a hurricane of thoughts. Someone had tried to kill my father and my girlfriend. I was pulled in different directions, not knowing whom to save first. While I had Michaela safe at home for now, I would continue with my purpose here today and seek out one of the professors. Once we knew what Michaela was for certain, perhaps that information would save them both.

I picked up my phone and dialed Leo's number.

He answered after the first ring. "Hello?"

"Why didn't you tell me what happened in the dungeons?" I demanded.

"I was taking care of it, and I didn't think you needed to be pulled away from your other focus right now," he explained.

"I need you to find out who helped him escape. Review the surveillance videos from the kingdom. Let's hope he shows his face," I said.

Jenkins snapped his head up and grinned.

"Yes, I'm on it," said Leo.

"Leo, who's with my father right now?" I asked.

"I believe my mother and Uncle Theodore," he said. The words did not comfort me.

"Ask Aunt Olympia to sit with him until I get home. Tell her I think it's important for her to do so." Aunt Olympia was the only person in my family who'd tried to think of a way to help my father. She was the only one I trusted right now.

"I'll tell her. Anything else?" he asked.

"That's it for now," I said and ended the call.

After a few long, deep breaths, I mentally left my anger and frustration in that dirty dungeon and exited toward the hallway. I walked past the library and made my way to the academy.

In addition to any public school they attended, manticores had to take classes at our academy when they reached the age of maturity. In our kingdom, that age was thirteen.

It was an age of self-awareness, an age when we felt our greater strength and our predator needs. Many of us questioned who we were and our purpose in the world around this age. Our professors helped guide our youth and offered strategies to curb our violent instincts, so we could all live our lives freely among the earth's other inhabitants.

The first manticores lived in jungles and hunted animals. They fought among themselves for power and fed off vulnerable prey. For centuries they roamed the world feeding their predatory needs. But as we evolved, our intellect grew, and we wanted to be more than just predators. Unfortunately, around the Middle Ages, a few manticores could not control their instincts, and stories of these horrific beasts circulated in villages. Manticores were hunted and forced to live in the shadows.

My grandfather was the first to train others to control their anger and their need to dominate. A few even fell in love. My grandfather was one of those manticores who came to the heartbreaking realization that intimacy with humans would be fatal for them. No matter how well he learned to control his instincts, he could never change the poison within his body.

In my most indecisive moments, I always came back to my professors for advice and strategies. They had spent decades working to help manticores be more than beasts, more than predators, more than killers.

There were private offices in this quarter of the kingdom. Many were held by the kingdom's professors. I knocked on Professor Wallace's door. He was one of my favorites.

I remembered a time when I had just begun my manticore classes. I was a tall but skinny boy, not quite developed yet. The other boys picked on me, and I fought back. I never won but I held my own. After one particularly brutal fight Professor Wallace had broken up, he pulled me aside and told me that my greatest weakness wasn't my lack of muscles but my strategy. "Knowledge is power, and power is knowing how to use your strengths," he'd said.

He'd taught me a few strategies to use my height to my advantage and my quickness to defend myself the next time. We both knew there would be a next time. It was inevitable because the instinct to dominate was innately strong within us. We couldn't change that instinct, but we could change the outcome, he'd told me. In the end, I'd proven I could take care of myself—many times without even throwing a punch.

That's why I came to him first. He knew how to use knowledge as a weapon, and today knowledge was my greatest ally.

Before I could knock, I heard someone walk up to the door and open it. Professor Wallace stood on the other side. Since we manticores did not age quickly, Professor Wallace looked exactly as he did all those years ago.

"Hunter, nice to see you," he said with a jovial smile.

"Professor Wallace, it is great to see you, as well," I replied.

"Please, come in." He motioned me inside with his arm. I sat in front of his desk. I felt like a thirteen-year-old boy again but shook the feeling off. I had more than some bullies on my back today; these opponents were killers.

"What can I do for you?" he asked.

"I'm here because I've discovered some tomes in old Italian that I cannot confidently decipher," I explained. "It's important I understand them, as I believe they hold the answers I'm searching for."

"All right, let me see what you have there," he said and held out his hand.

I unlocked the briefcase and pulled out the book. It was the largest one I'd found in the trunks, and I'd thought perhaps it would be the best one to start with. I handed it to Professor Wallace.

He felt the leather around the book, brought it closer to his nose and inhaled deeply. He took a moment as he turned it over in his hands. It looked as if he was appraising the book.

He then turned to the first page, sat down and began to read. I sat and watched him as he turned page after page. I did not move, using all of my patience to quietly wait.

After reading what looked to be about twenty or thirty pages, Professor Wallace glanced up at me.

"Where did you find this book?" he asked.

"I cannot say right now," I told him. The fewer who knew about Michaela, the better.

"Well, I have heard of the existence of these books, but I don't know if any manticore has ever laid eyes on one," he said.

"So, you know what it is?" I asked, hearing the hope in my voice.

"I cannot be sure, as I've only just begun reading it, but I believe these are writings from The Sheds."

"The Sheds?"

"Yes," he said. I waited for him to explain, but he didn't.

"Professor, who are The Sheds?" I asked.

He looked over my head and stood up to close his door.

"Shed was an Egyptian god. He was known as 'the protector,' 'the enchanter,' or 'he who rescues.' It's been said he had the ability to master wild beasts of the desert and river as well as poisonous creatures such as snakes, spiders, and scorpions. There were stories of how he provided his people protection from the animals as well as from any illness that would develop from coming into contact with them. Unlike some of the other Egyptian gods that were worshipped in a temple, Shed was worshipped among the people. Ordinary Egyptians turned to him for their everyday needs, to save their children from illness, their loved ones from misfortune and even death.

"Over the years, I have heard tales of how his intercession could lengthen a person's time in this world, or save a person's soul from the underworld, even providing a substitute in his place.

"Shed, the god, was male. It says in this book that he mated with the daughter of the Sun god Ra. Their union produced only female descendants. These descendants are known as The Sheds. They are said to have the same powers as their father. Some say they are even stronger."

"Do these descendants have any distinguishing features?" I asked, thoughts rioting in my head.

Professor Wallace raised an eyebrow at me, and I felt as if he could read my thoughts.

"As a matter of fact, I've heard that they do. The Sheds are said to have purple eyes. Have you happened to read anything referencing those with purple eyes?" he asked me. I got the feeling he already knew the answer.

"I have. I went to our library and read whatever I could find but there wasn't much there," I explained.

"What did you find?" he asked.

"Just one story, a folklore. It described a young woman who defeated a beast with long nails and fangs with only a song."

He smiled at this. "I'm impressed, Hunter. Not many people have searched and fewer still have found the story. Some at the academy wanted to tear the page from the book, *Folk Stories Untold*."

"Why?"

"Because people—and manticores too—are fearful of what they do not know," he said. "We have never made the connection between those with violet eyes and The Sheds, but we have been around long enough to put the stories together and suspect it."

I shook my head, so he continued.

"The folklore does not mention the particular god, but it does say Violet gets her power from the gods. The book you just allowed me to briefly skim through confirms that The Sheds are descendants of the Egyptian god Shed. It was extraordinary to read. It said that whenever a child of his was born, Shed and his wife would light up the night sky violet in her honor."

"Why is this the first time I'm hearing of The Sheds, Professor?" I wondered.

"At first, rumors about The Sheds were only stories that mothers told their children at night so they listened and stayed in line. Those stories were similar to Violet's, where a woman slayed the manticore. But then rumors began to circulate that The Sheds could heal manticores and not just humans. However, no one—in our kingdom, at least—had actually encountered a Shed descendant," he explained. "If someone encountered a being with violet eyes, they found her to have no special ability, only some pleasing characteristics, and she perhaps tended to live longer than the average human."

He pulled out another book, this one from his own shelf.

"But, about fifty or sixty years ago, there were stories of a Shed woman who lived in Algeria. She was considered a wise woman who could heal those with 'satanic' wounds, bite marks that could not be traced back to a human or animal. We assumed these wounds were made by a rogue manticore. The bite marks were smaller than that of a lion's but deadlier. While the villagers stopped the bleeding, the victim still died. Since the wound didn't puncture an organ or an artery, presumably the poison killed them. This was consistent with a manticore attack. Of course, this type of behavior was outlawed. But by the time your father's people investigated, the victims who'd survived, presumably healed by the Shed woman, had no recollection of the attack. By then, the Shed woman was gone too. There was no evidence that any healing or attack had even occurred. All that was left were stories."

Professor Wallace placed the book back on his shelf and took a seat at his desk again.

"Since there have not been many cases over the centuries, we don't really talk about it here at the academy. We don't want to give the students false information, so until we know more, we prefer not to mention it. We wouldn't want to get scores of manticores hunting these women if they knew they had the ability to heal manticores, save souls, and who knows what else."

"You're right. A weapon like that would be coveted and would even start wars," I said.

"Indeed. If The Sheds truly do have the power the stories claim they do, they could be the most powerful creatures on this earth. What a weapon that would be in the hands of the wrong enemy."

"Do you know how they wield this power?" I asked.

"I do not. However, just from the little I've read in this book, it may be through chants, meditation and prayers taught from generation to generation," he said.

"So, you think these books could be like spell books?" I asked, trying to make sense of all this.

"No, The Sheds are not witches. They are descendants of gods. They are much more powerful than witches or spells. As the descendants of Ra, they grow their power through light, not darkness nor dark arts."

Descendants of Ra, the Sun god, the god of light. Michaela's grandmother's name was Ramona. Her mother was Lucia, a derivative of *luce*, meaning *light* in Italian. Even Michaela could be named after the archangel Michael. He was always depicted with a drawn sword, ready to fight, and often with his foot crushing a serpent. Michaela could be the greatest warrior in the world without needing to wield a sword. She could make and destroy kings and she didn't even know it. How was I to tell her this? How would she take the information? Would she even believe me?

"What would you do if you encountered a Shed?" I asked, seeking my professor's advice.

He stared at me and seemed to assume, correctly, that I had already found her.

"I would not tell a soul. If I cared about this woman, I would protect her identity. I suspect this is why we haven't heard of many Shed women. It would be suicide to reveal oneself, and murder to identify one. She would be a prize worth killing for."

His words both scared and ignited me. A fire burned in my soul to protect Michaela, even from my family. If there was a traitor among us, he would not stop at killing the king, especially when a bigger prize was to be gained.

"Thank you, Professor," I said as I reached for the book.

"May I keep it a little longer?" he asked, still holding it tightly in his hands. "I don't know if I will ever have the opportunity to read one like it again. I will keep it secret, of course. But if there's anything further to be learned, I will send you a message."

I contemplated this. I didn't think it would put Michaela at risk if he were to read more of the book. It did not mention her, of course, as it had been written well before her time. Perhaps if the professor could discover more information about The Sheds, their powers, and perhaps their weaknesses, I could better protect her.

"You may keep it, for a little while longer. In fact, I'd like you to take note of ways The Sheds can protect themselves," I said.

He nodded in understanding. "I will be happy to do this for you and for her."

I thought to deny that I knew of any Shed woman, but I realized how futile the attempt would be. "Thank you, Professor, but I really must go now," I said and opened the door.

"Hunter," he called out, and I turned around.

"Yes?"

"If she is discovered, power-hungry manticores won't stop until they have her," he warned.

"Let them come," I said. "I'll be ready."

Twenty-Five

Hunter

After I left the kingdom, I went straight to my father's home. I needed to tell Michaela everything I knew. I pulled into the long driveway and parked my car in the garage.

I jogged up the front steps and paused in the foyer to think where she would be. First, I searched for her in my old bedroom where we had slept the night before. Someone had made the bed, but the room was now empty. I frowned at not finding her there, but I continued my search. In the short time I had known Michaela, I knew her to be selfless. So the next place I checked was my father's room. When I opened the door, my father was sleeping peacefully in his bed. My aunt Olympia sat next to him but I didn't see Michaela.

"Hunter, you're back," said Aunt Olympia. "Did you find the answers you were looking for?"

"Yes and no," I said hesitantly. "A professor at the university is taking a look now and may know more in a few days."

"Oh," she said and looked away to caress my father's hand. Aunt Olympia cared for my father; my instincts were not wrong there.

"Do you know where I can find Michaela?" I asked my aunt.

"She said she was heading to the sunroom to read," she responded. "She left only a little while ago. She may still be there."

"Thank you," I said and turned to leave.

"Hunter?" she called out to me.

"Yes?"

"Are you any closer to finding out who tried to kill your father?" she asked.

"Not yet," I said. "But I will. I promise you, I will."

She nodded once and smoothed out the bed linens. I closed the door and headed for the sunroom.

Michaela sat in an upholstered chair that had once belonged to King Louis VIII. My grandfather had taken it from the king's palace centuries ago. He'd claimed it was a gift from the king, but my father said he probably fancied it and simply took the chair from Louis. The French king would not have stopped him.

Michaela hadn't noticed me yet. I'd found the door open, so I hadn't made a sound yet. I watched her for a moment before I made my presence known. Her dark hair reflected the light and looked iridescent basking in the sun. Her skin beckoned—soft and smooth. Her posture, despite being curled in a chair, held an undeniable grace and elegance. How had I missed it? How had I not known she was a goddess? The evidence stared at me. But could she heal bodies and save souls? I shook my head. The thought humbled me and, at the same time, scared me to death.

"Michaela?" I called out, before I lost the courage to speak with her.

She turned her head toward me, and her smile lit me up from the inside, like it always did.

"Hunter! You're back," she said and rose from her chair.

"No, stay. I think it's better if you sit," I explained.

"Do you have bad news?" she asked. Concern spilled out in her voice.

"It's not necessarily bad news," I said, although I worried bad people would materialize because of it. "As you know, I brought the book to our professors. I brought it to one in particular, and he read it."

"He did? That's wonderful," she said, her concern now replaced with exuberance. She saw the hesitation on my face. "What's wrong?" she asked.

"Michaela, I don't know how much of this is true, but I will tell you everything he told me. Mind you, he could not verify it, only told me what he'd heard." I prefaced the professor's stories with as much caution as possible. I then recounted everything Professor Wallace had said in his private office.

"So, you see, there is no evidence of the Shed woman or of any of the victims. All we have are stories," I finished and waited for her response. I expected tears, anger, fear...anything...except laughter. She bent forward, howling her amusement. I worried her outburst was a prelude to a breakdown of some sort, but then I realized she was genuinely amused.

"That is the most ridiculous thing I've ever heard," she said.

I didn't know how to respond. So, she continued.

"Hunter, I know you are an educated man, and I don't mean to imply your professors are ridiculous. He's just recounting folklore, he can't believe any of this, can he?"

Again, I wanted to tread carefully. "He didn't want to confirm or deny their existence, having not met a Shed himself, but he didn't dismiss the possibility, no."

"Come on, Hunter, really? People used to believe in fairies and exorcisms and that the earth was flat. We know that none of those are real. The books in my parents' home were probably just old books that depicted some type of witchcraft," she said.

"He was pretty adamant that it wasn't witchcraft," I said.

"Well, whatever it is, it isn't something I need to worry about. I don't have any magical healing abilities. If I did, I would march upstairs right now and heal your father. I know you want this to be true, but I'm not a Shed or, good grief, a goddess. Tricia would pee herself laughing at this one."

"You cannot tell anyone what I just told you, Michaela," I said.

"Promise me." I instilled every ounce of my fear into my voice to show her how serious I was. She looked at me curiously and then asked, "Why do you believe this could be true?"

"Because things such as fairies and witchcraft are not necessarily untrue," I said, again choosing my words carefully. She no longer laughed but did not look convinced.

"Are you saying you believe in these things?" she asked.

"Yes, I do," I said.

"Have you ever met a fairy or a witch?" she asked with a smirk.

"Yes, I have," I confirmed.

Her face grew serious. "Are you a witch?" she asked.

Now I couldn't help but laugh. "My God, don't be ridiculous," I said.

"I don't think I'm the one being ridiculous," she countered.

If I couldn't get her to take Professor Wallace's words seriously, she may not heed his warning of danger either. I had to make her understand.

"Michaela, I know this is a lot to take in, especially from someone who's lived her whole life in the twenty-first century, where such matters are discussed only by the fringe of society. It is supposed to be that way. Those who do not want to be discovered want to keep it that way. So, I don't blame you for not taking this seriously at first. But you must start now. You must open your mind to the possibility that humans and animals are not the only creatures on this earth. Forget what you've been taught. Open your eyes and see what's in front of your face."

She stopped laughing, and she stared at me instead.

I shut my eyes and allowed my predatory instincts to kick in. I inhaled. The scent of her skin travelled through my nostrils and down my throat until a growl rose from deep within my chest. I opened my eyes and gave them free rein to show the extent of my desire to overtake her.

My chest heaved from the anticipation of the chase. Her eyes grew bigger as she took in my lion-like pupils. A low growl resounded from my lips. She not only saw but heard the changes in me. She likely felt it too. I smelled her fear and sensed as my incisors lengthened. I tasted the venom leaking in my mouth. It was in her nature to run when she stood before such danger, so I anticipated her motion to flee and caught her in my arms before she could get away. She panted and pushed against my hold, fear undoubtedly racing in her veins. She was like a fly caught in a spider's web.

I shut my eyes again and breathed deeply. I regained control by slowing down my breaths and calming my instincts. I reminded myself she was not prey.

I knew she felt the change in me when her arms went limp in my grasp.

"Don't be afraid. I won't hurt you," I said while I continued to hold her. After a few seconds, I let go of one arm to caress her wrist with my thumb, back and forth. I didn't attempt any more affection than that. I didn't think she trusted me yet.

Good, she shouldn't trust someone like me.

"Michaela, I am going to let go of you now. Promise me you're not going to run," I said.

She didn't move and hardly took a breath. I tried to reassure her again.

"I'm in control of myself. I promise, I won't hurt you."

"Okay," she said softly, but I heard it.

All right. This was it. I loosened my grip on her wrists and let go of her. I waited for her to look at me. She didn't. She stared at the ground instead.

"Please, look at me," I begged.

My instincts were under control, and I was confident my eyes reflected that. She looked up. She didn't look scared anymore, and I was pleased with my ability to rein in my instincts on command.

"What the hell was that?" she shouted and smacked my arm.

I smiled because she sounded angry now and not scared. I preferred angry.

"I still cannot tell you what I am, but I need you to understand that things are not always what they seem. Other beings do exist in this world, despite society not accepting it."

"And you are one of those other beings," she asked hesitantly.

I nodded once.

"Are you a vampire?" she whispered.

I could have taken the easy route and lied, but I didn't want to do that to her.

"No," I said.

She nodded again. "Okay, good. I get queasy at the sight of blood, and as much as I'd love to run fast, I couldn't handle drinking blood."

I was confused, then understanding dawned. "Michaela, you cannot become what I am. It is not something that can be passed onto someone else. You are either born this way or not."

"But it doesn't prevent us from being together, does it?" she asked, ready to take on something she didn't fully understand yet.

"It sort of does, at least in the biblical sense," I said, and it broke my heart to see her bright face darken.

"Why not?"

"Because any kind of intimacy between us could kill you, Michaela, and I would never risk that," I said. Finally able to express my biggest fear to her. It felt good to have this out in the open between us.

She didn't say anything but paced the room.

"If you tell me that I should believe in more than I've been told to believe in, in more than what I can see with my eyes, then why can you not do the same? Why not believe that we can be together?" she asked.

I opened my mouth to answer, but then realized I didn't know how to respond to that. *Because it's never been done before? Never* wasn't impossible.

Her determination refueled mine. I, too, wanted to believe we could be together. I swore that we would be. But we had to be careful and not rush into anything until we knew more.

"I don't know for sure. Because a Shed has never been with...with...someone like me before."

"So, we don't know for sure that we cannot be together," she reiterated with a smile, knowing I had to concede to this statement.

"No, we don't know for sure," I said, smiling back.

"Good. We will find a way," she reminded me.

This time I nodded because the words were stuck in my throat. I was in awe of this woman. She was fearless, timeless, and truly a goddess.

"If I am to believe I am a healer, then I must try with your father," she told me. "You said The Sheds' ability to heal was through prayer, meditation, and chants?"

"Yes, that is what Professor Wallace said," I confirmed.

"Well, I tried prayer and that may have helped. But it wasn't enough. I don't know any chants but perhaps I can try meditation." She continued pacing across the room, her hands clasped in front of her chest while she walked back and forth.

"What sort of meditation?" I asked.

"Well, I'm no expert, but I've heard of various forms of meditation, and one of them is called loving-kindness meditation or 'metta' meditation. It's about sending good vibes, warmth, and kindness toward others. I'll try to send healing too. I don't know if it will work, but I will try," she said.

"Thank you," I whispered.

She walked out of the room and I followed her, like her loyal subject.

We walked up the stairs, and I took them two at a time to catch up with her. She was determined to help, and I loved this about her. But most of all I loved her.

I grabbed her hand and held it in mine. It felt small in my much larger palm, but in no way did I find her weaker. No, Michaela was the strongest person I knew. And she was mine.

I couldn't stop the smile that broke across my face. For the first time, I allowed hope to enter my consciousness, allowed it to grow in my heart.

When we reached my father's room, I noticed Aunt Elenora and Leo had joined Aunt Olympia. I pulled Michaela back, stopping her from entering the room.

"Michaela, no one else must know what we suspect you to be," I warned.

"Why not?" she asked.

Michaela would not simply do as she was told, like everyone else around me. She needed to understand why. It wasn't about taking orders—it was about reconciling them.

"Professor Wallace cautioned me that there are those who would want to wield your powers, wield you like a weapon," I reminded her.

"Yes, but this does not apply to your family," she countered.

"I wish I could say that with certainty, but I cannot." I was not used to explaining myself, but I would try to for her. I kept my voice low in case another manticore was nearby. "Before I met with Professor Wallace, I had to see about some trouble with a criminal." She nodded, probably trying to process everything. "He warned me that the traitor may be close to me. I don't know if he wanted to mess with my head or if he was telling the truth. Either way, I won't risk putting you in danger."

"You think your aunt or cousin could have tried to kill your father?" she asked.

"I don't know. At this point, anyone could be a suspect. I trust no one," I said. I would watch the video footage before I ruled anyone out completely.

"But me," she responded.

"But you. And Aunt Olympia. I trust her too."

"Okay. I understand, Hunter," she said. She then asked, "You said your father was poisoned, right?"

"Yes."

"I will focus my meditation on flushing the poison away from his organs. I will visualize it leaving his body and being replaced with clean, healthy blood."

I nodded and led her into the room.

Aunt Elenora and Leo looked up when we came in, but Aunt Olympia's focus remained on my father.

"You're back," said Leo.

"Yes," I replied.

"Would it be okay if I sit there beside him?" Michaela asked Aunt Olympia. Olympia looked up at me for permission. I gave a slight nod of approval. She rose from her chair.

"Thank you," said Michaela and sat down next to my father. She picked up his hand, closed her eyes, but did not say a word.

"What is she doing?" asked Aunt Elenora.

"She is sitting with my father," I said.

I knew she wanted to say more but thought better of pushing me.

"Leo, can I see you outside?" I motioned for Leo to follow me out into the hallway. He waited for me to go first and then walked behind me.

Once we were in the hallway, I got straight to the point.

"Did you check the surveillance videos?" I asked.

"I did. I could see a figure wearing a long black coat, a broad hat and dark glasses walking toward the cell," said Leo.

"None of the guards thought wearing sunglasses underground was suspicious?" I asked.

"He didn't put the sunglasses on until he was alone in the dungeons. He also had his back toward the camera before he put the glasses on, so we did not see his face," Leo explained. "It was either all a great coincidence or this man knew exactly where the cameras were and how to avoid them."

"We need to check the cameras here in the house," I said. "It could be the same person helping Jenkins and trying to kill the king."

"But it's only been family at the house in the last couple of weeks. We've had no meetings or guests. Do you really think it's worth checking the cameras?" Leo asked.

A shiver of unease crawled up my spine. Was Leo trying to avoid looking at the cameras in the house? Was there something he was hiding?

"Yes, I think it's worth taking a look. I'll take a look at them with you. Pull up everything, all angles from each room, starting from two days before the poisoning," I said.

Leo whistled, "That's going to be a lot of footage but all right. I'll get on it."

He walked away toward the security room, and I watched him go for a minute before I joined him. I hated suspecting my family, but with no other leads, I couldn't ignore this one.

With my father dead and me out of the way, Aunt Elenora would be the next in line for the throne. If she were to order it, she could make Leo not only the heir but one of the most powerful manticores in the kingdom. He would no longer have to take orders but would be the one to give them. *But would he kill for it?* I needed to be ready in case that proved to be true.

Twenty-Six

Hunter

Leo and I watched the surveillance tapes for hours. As he said, there were no guests in the home, only family and the usual security staff. No one entered my father's chamber from the hallway or lingered near his door to check if he was sleeping. Everything looked fine. We did not see anything suspicious. It was maddening.

What am I missing? Is something hidden from these camera angles?

The assailant knew how to hide from the cameras in the dungeons; obviously he'd done the same here. If he were aware of the camera positions, he could easily avoid detection.

I put myself in the position of the assassin. How would I get away with murder? A careful plan, an escape route, an alibi.

An escape route. Wait.

A memory wormed its way through my mind. I played with my cousins, running away from them, and then hiding. I hated to lose and so I hid in the secret passageway my father had shown me earlier that year. I'd promised him I would tell no one about it, but I didn't think anyone would find me there. Unfortunately, the dust from the tunnel made me sneeze and Leo and the boys found me behind the hidden door.

I stood up and headed for my mother's old bedroom, where the secret passageway door was hidden. Leo noticed me leave, but I didn't wait for him to follow. My heart raced now. I didn't know if it was from fear that I was right, or anticipation that I knew who the traitor was.

I ran down the hallway to the last door, and entered my mother's old bedroom. I scanned the room. It remained exactly as she'd left it. Her silver brush and mirror still sat on her dressing table. Her hats and scarves hung on the wall. Her bed remained perfectly made, and the pillows stood tall and straight. The passageway door was not easily visible; it blended in with the wood paneling, but I knew where to look for it. It had been a very long time since I'd used it.

I walked up to the door and turned the handle that was neatly embedded in the wood. The door was unlocked. My heart nearly jumped out of my chest. I didn't know what I expected to happen, but my instincts told me I would find something here.

I opened the door all the way and it only took a moment for my eyes to adjust to the darkness. I inspected the tunnel ahead, but I didn't see anything unusual. Maybe I was wrong. Maybe there was nothing here.

I stepped forward and walked toward the end of the tunnel. It was at least two hundred feet to the other side. I recalled it being muddy on that end because of the nearby stream. Maybe I would find a footprint near the water.

I took another step, and that's when I felt something. I looked down and lying on the dirty ground at my feet was a shoe—a man's running shoe.

I turned in a circle, looking for the other shoe, but there was just the one. I picked it up and examined it. I didn't remember seeing this exact shoe on anyone, but there were only a couple of people who knew of this secret passageway.

"Hunter, what is it?" I heard Leo's voice. It came from inside the bedroom.

Speak of the devil and he shall appear.

"Did you find something?" he asked.

I did. "I found something, Leo," I said, my voice even. I didn't trust my control right now.

"Well, what is it?" he asked.

I emerged from the tunnel and brandished the shoe as if it were a knife.

"Where is the other one, Leo?" I asked softly.

"What?" Leo looked confused, but he was a good actor. I had seen him lie countless times to his mother.

"What are you talking about? Did you find that shoe in the passageway?" he asked.

"Is the other shoe still in my father's room?" I responded.

This time my voice grew louder, but I didn't care. I stormed across the bedroom and opened the door to the dressing room. It was empty. I spied the adjoining door that led to my father's bedroom. I turned my neck to stare at Leo. *This must be how he avoided the security cameras.* He knew there weren't any cameras in the bedrooms or dressing rooms. The passageway not only ensured his entry but also that he wouldn't be detected.

"Where is it, Leo?" I shouted at him as I charged into my father's bedroom.

I startled Michaela and Aunt Olympia, who were both in the room. Michaela still held my father's hand. His pale, weak hand incited my anger. This time, I barely held on to my control. My hands curled into fists, and I sucked in ragged breaths.

"I don't know what you are talking about, Hunter," Leo said. This time, his voice got louder too.

The commotion attracted a few more people to the scene. Aunt Elenora, Uncle Theodore, and John entered my father's chambers.

Good, this may be the only trial Leo got before I tore him apart.

"What's this all about?" asked Uncle Theodore.

"I found this shoe in the hidden passageway. The one that leads directly into my father's chamber. The one that avoids the hallways and the cameras," I said, enunciating each word, so everyone understood my meaning.

"There's no secret passageway," said Uncle Theodore.

"There is, Uncle, and Leo knew about it," I said.

"Yes, I knew about it, but I've never used it. And that is not my shoe. It's not even stylish," he said a bit too flippantly. It angered me more.

"I'm going to give you three seconds to tell me why you did it before I rip your throat out," I growled.

"No!" shouted Aunt Elenora. She realized the authenticity of my threat. "Hunter, it wasn't Leo. It couldn't have been."

"Of course, it wasn't, Mother. I would not commit treason," he said, and then to me he added, "I can't believe you could consider such a thing, Hunter."

"Put the shoe on," I demanded.

"What?" Leo asked.

"I said: Put. The. Shoe. On," I repeated, and I tossed it at him.

The shoe landed with a soft thud at his feet.

Leo gave an exaggerated huff but picked up the shoe and untied the laces. When I saw him easily slide his foot inside the sneaker and that the shoe fit, I lost the last stitch of my self-control. I went straight for his neck.

Twenty-Seven

Michaela

I had been sitting with Hunter's father for the past couple of hours meditating. Olympia sat with me the whole time. It drained me, but I didn't want to give up just yet. When I first imagined the poison flowing through his body, I swore I could taste it. At first, there was a pervasive metallic flavor in my mouth, but after a few minutes it was gone. Only a sour aftertaste remained.

Olympia had encouraged me with her soft smile when I looked up at her. I grew tired, but she had to be tired too, so I went on.

I visualized his blood flowing like a rushing river through his veins. I imagined it pushing all the poison away from his organs and into his gallbladder, where the bile would break it down until it disintegrated. I had no medical background to know if the gallbladder could do such a thing, but that was the route my mind took so I went with it.

As I meditated, I sensed something different with Hunter's father. His heart sped up to more than twice its usual speed and then abruptly stopped beating. I panicked, worried I'd done something wrong. I held his wrist, checking for a pulse, when he took in a loud gasp of air. The sound frightened me, and I let go of his hand. His mouth remained open for a few seconds and closed on the exhale. Then, he went back to sleep.

I placed my two fingers at his neck and felt a strong and steady heartbeat. His breathing sounded deeper too, but he remained unconscious.

Olympia stared at me with eyes larger than an owl's. I'd wanted to tell her I needed a break when Hunter stormed through the room. He held in his hand what looked like an old sneaker. A second later, Leo trailed in behind him.

Hunter shouted at Leo. He sounded angry—angrier than I had ever seen him. It frightened me. He took deep breaths to control his anger but was losing the battle.

Then others entered the room.

I tried to listen.

Hunter accused Leo of poisoning his father!

Oh my God, that can't be true.

It would destroy Hunter to know his cousin was the traitor. Even though he suspected it could be family, the proof of it would be too much.

I reached for Hunter to try and calm him down and get to the bottom of this, when I froze. Hunter crouched down close to the floor, in what I could only describe as a predator position, poised to strike. He shot out and leaped onto Leo with his teeth bared. I couldn't move, couldn't believe what I saw.

Leo did not back down. The growl that emerged from him scared me to my core. It was an unnatural sound, like an unworldly roar, that made the hair on the back of my neck stand on end.

Hunter swiped at Leo with his hand. I blinked twice because I could not have possibly seen claws replace Hunter's fingernails.

Dear God, what is he?

Hunter bared his teeth once again and this time connected with Leo's shoulder. Leo shouted out in pain but didn't go down.

"No, stop! Stop this!" shouted Elenora.

"What is happening?" I asked Olympia.

"Someone get her out of here!" yelled Theodore. "She cannot be a witness to this!"

"No," I said. I didn't want to leave and not know what would happen to Hunter.

Olympia stood by my side next to the bed and held me in her arms. I was so thankful for the embrace, since I thought my legs would crumble at any moment. Her support also signaled she would not get rid of me, and I hugged her back for it.

I covered my ears with my hands to protect me from the sounds of fabric tearing and inhuman voices snarling. I did not hear Hunter's father speak. But I did see, from the corner of my eye, his hand raised just a few inches off of the bed, and then his lips moved.

"He's trying to speak," I said to Olympia, and she loosened her hold on me as I crouched myself down beside Hunter's father.

"It…it…" was all I could hear him say. I held his hand and put my ear to his lips.

A lamp crashed beside me as Hunter threw Leo across the room. Leo landed on his back on top of the table.

"Say it again," I pleaded with him. "Please, say it once more."

He opened his eyes and looked directly into mine. "It…it…was…John," he said with what looked like every ounce of strength he could muster. And then shut his eyes once again.

I felt numb from the revelation. I tried to wrap my head around the words and their meaning. I was sure he'd tried to tell me who had attempted to kill him, and it wasn't Leo. It was John. Who stood in this very room.

I didn't know what to do. Did I say something now and risk John attacking me, or wait until I had Hunter alone?

Another crash. This time one of the sets of knight's armor that hung on the wall came crashing down on top of Hunter, and it momentarily distracted him. Leo pounced, his lips curled up exposing his fangs. If Leo killed Hunter now, I wouldn't get the chance to tell him what his father had revealed. Hunter would be dead. I shouted as loud as I could.

"Stop!" I screamed. "Your father is awake!"

It worked. Everyone in the room, including Leo and Hunter, were frozen in place.

"No, he's not," said Theodore, looking down at Hunter's father, whose eyes were still closed.

"He was," I said and then took a deep breath. "He told me who the traitor is."

"He what?" Leo said, disbelief in his voice.

"Michaela," said Hunter. "What are you saying?"

"Your father spoke, he even opened his eyes momentarily," I explained. "He said a name, and I think he was trying to tell me who poisoned him."

"What did he say?" Hunter asked, raising himself up from the ground, his chest rising and falling from exertion.

"He said it was John," I said in a low voice, but I suspected everyone heard me.

No one uttered a word. The room went deathly silent. I was scared all over again, only this time for myself.

"What is this? What are you up to? My son did not try to kill the king," sputtered Theodore. "How dare you say such a thing. If you simply wanted to distract Hunter from being killed, well, you've done it. Now take back what you've just implied."

"I didn't imply it. That is what he said." I stood tall even though my legs felt numb.

"Ridiculous," said Elenora.

"I heard it too," said Olympia, surprising me with her statement. Hunter's father had spoken softly but Olympia heard. Whatever they were, they must have a keen sense of hearing.

"John?" This time it was Leo who raised himself up from the

ground. I heard the confusion laced in his voice. "John, what do you say to this?"

Everyone in the room stared at the accused man. He hadn't spoken yet to confirm or deny the accusation.

His chest heaved and he panted out his breaths. His face was blotchy and sweaty. He looked as angry as Hunter had moments ago. Now Hunter simply looked shocked. His face was blank of expression.

"John knew about the hidden passageway too," said Leo. "He played with us when we were kids. He knew it was here."

John nodded his head but didn't say anything.

"That is your shoe, isn't it?" asked Leo.

"I knew the passageway would be muddy. I didn't want to leave any tracks," said John. His voice was even but his breathing was hectic.

Leo's mouth hung open at John's admission. He stepped forward, his hands curled into fists and shouted, "How could you try to kill the king!"

Hunter didn't speak, but I couldn't take my eyes off of him. The silence felt as deadly as his teeth just moments ago.

"Why, John?" Hunter finally asked.

John opened his mouth, about to say something, but then looked down and shook his head. He kept shaking it, barely holding himself together.

"You tampered with the antidote, didn't you?" Hunter asked as he approached John. "You're the reason why the physician couldn't get it to work."

"This is absurd," said Theodore standing between Hunter and his son. "John, tell them how you couldn't possibly be the one who tried to kill the king."

John raised his head and stared at the ceiling. He growled and pinned his father with his eyes.

"Why, Father?" John lashed out. "Because I am not smart enough to devise such a plan? Because I am not strong enough to execute it? Because I am not loyal enough to understand what needs to be done. Well, I am all of those things."

"Yes, and a traitor too," said Hunter, softly. But John heard him.

"I am not the one who is the traitor to our people," John sneered at Hunter. "I am not the one who seeks to repress who we are, who we are meant to be. We are the stronger ones, the worthier ones. We will not be some neutered animals."

Something John said must've registered with Hunter because his head snapped up.

"What did you say?" he asked. When John took a step back and didn't respond, Hunter continued. "It was you. You were the one working with Jenkins. You were the one who tried to release him. You don't deny it, do you?"

"I do not," he said in a proud voice.

"Did you know he was attacking those people?" Hunter asked.

"Humans? Who cares? But no, I didn't know him when he was on the streets. After he was captured, we came up with a plan. I struck a deal with him. I told him, if he convinced your father that he could be rehabilitated, then I would free him. He agreed. We knew this would be the perfect event to incite a revolution. You saw for yourself in that courtroom, there are others who would rather have seen Jenkins hang."

"You said 'we'," Hunter said softly.

John stuttered and surveyed those in the room. But then he brought his attention back to Hunter. "I meant me...and Jenkins."

"Did you? Or did you mean another accomplice?" Hunter asked.

"I did it all on my own. I didn't need anyone else's help."

"For what purpose, John?" Hunter implored.

"Aren't you listening?" he shouted this time. "You and your father are not strong enough to lead us through to the next evolution. Your father speaks of justice, but it is not the law of the land he seeks to maintain. It's the laws set by humans, those inferior to us. And you, you are no better. You are too soft to lead us into battle, to secure our rule on this earth. You don't want to fight humans," he said with an awful sneer and then looked at me. "You want to fuck them."

A roar reverberated across the room and shook the rafters. I covered my ears again but kept my eyes open. Hunter roared and balled his fists, seconds before he leaped across the bed and pinned John to the ground.

Hunter snapped his teeth, but John evaded him each time. He pushed Hunter off and got into a fighter's stance. Hunter stood up, too, but didn't waste any time getting John back down. With a punch to the gut and a kick to the face, John fell once again to the floor. Hunter continued to kick him hard, in the ribs, in the stomach, and then on his temple.

"No!" shouted Theodore, and Elenora held him back.

John didn't stay down though; he got up. Hunter and John circled each other, both waiting for the other to make the next move. Theodore reached for Hunter's arm. The movement distracted Hunter and gave John the opportunity to wrap his claws around Hunter's neck.

"No!" I screamed and my stomach dropped when Hunter's face contorted. His mouth opened wide, but he couldn't breathe. He clawed at John's hands and blood dripped between his fingers. John hissed but didn't loosen his grip.

Hunter slammed his foot onto John's instep, and he screamed. The pain caused John to momentarily release his grip, but it was enough time for Hunter to break free from his hold. Bent down, Hunter sucked in breath after breath, holding on to his throat. John roared and barrelled down on him. They wrestled on the floor, with John pummelling Hunter with punch after punch.

Hunter stretched out his neck and roared his frustration. He then snapped his teeth and reached for John's neck. John pushed Hunter away and stood up. Hunter raised himself off the ground but instead of attacking John, as I anticipated, he swiped his leg and John crashed to the floor and onto his back. Hunter stood in front of him and pressed his boot on John's throat.

I had this terrible feeling, like I'd seen this before. I remembered my dream at Aunt Julie's home and how scared I felt that Hunter would kill someone. I couldn't help the shout that tore through me, "Hunter," I screamed. "No, don't do it, please."

Hunter panted but didn't move. I couldn't tell if he had heard me. He only stared at John's face, which had turned purple.

"Don't do this," I said again. "You are not a killer."

He studied me then, his eyes still wild, but I was no longer afraid of him, only of what he would do.

He looked back down at John, and then lifted his foot away from John's throat and kicked his shoulder instead.

"Get him out of here," Hunter said to Leo. "Take him to the dungeon."

I ran to Hunter, and he caught me in his arms.

"It's over," he said into my hair, his deep breaths stirring the strands. "It's over."

Leo moved forward to pick John up, but John shoved his hand away. He got up on his own. He looked beaten but not defeated. He leaned forward, both hands on his knees, and continued to pant. He raised his head, and his eyes did not look wild like Hunter's. Instead, they looked terrifying. I'd heard the term *soulless* before, but I never thought I could see the void through someone's eyes. I saw it then.

He straightened up, pinned Hunter with his gaze and growled, "I will not be caged."

That's when I saw the knife.

John pulled off the leather cover and held it high above his head. He pulled the knife back, ready to throw it. I didn't know if he aimed the knife at me or at Hunter—all I knew was I had to stop him.

I wasn't as fast as Hunter, or strong enough to shove him out of the way, so I panicked. I screamed, "Stop" so loudly that my own ears rang.

I closed my eyes and screamed again, and this time I envisioned John stopping in his tracks. I envisioned his heart ceasing, then him dropping the knife to the ground.

Thump.

Then another scream. This one was not from me.

I opened my eyes, and John lay still on the ground.

I turned to look at Hunter. "What happened?"

He continued to stare at John's still body and did not respond right away. I pounded my fist on his chest. "What happened?" I shouted.

"He...he just froze. His eyes wide open. Dropped the knife onto the floor. Grabbed his chest, and then he fell to the ground."

Theodore and Elenora ran their hands along John's body, checking for a pulse, a heartbeat, anything.

"He's dead," said Elenora before glancing up at me.

"You killed him," whispered Theodore, then louder, "You killed my son!"

"I...I didn't touch him," I shouted back. "I didn't do anything."

"No, you did not touch him, but you killed him just the same," said Elenora calmly, but I didn't trust her tone. It sent a warning down my spine. "*What are you?*" she asked. Malice seeped through her voice.

"She is mine," said Hunter and grabbed my hand. "Get the physician to take a look at him—perhaps he is not dead. Michaela is coming with me."

And we exited the room, leaving what I was certain—although I had not touched him—was a dead man on the ground. God save me, I was a killer.

Twenty-Eight

Hunter

She was not a killer. She couldn't be. She hadn't even touched him. The last ten minutes replayed in my mind over and over, and I still could not comprehend what had happened. I led Michaela back to my room. Once I shut the door, I went to the closet and pulled out her suitcase.

"Michaela, you have to start packing. We need to leave immediately," I explained.

"Why?" she asked and moved to stand in front of me. I thought about lying but went with the truth instead, "Because you are no longer safe here."

"I didn't kill John," she said with tears in her eyes. "I couldn't have. I didn't even touch him. You have to explain to your family what I am, that I help people, not hurt them."

"I know you didn't mean to hurt him, but we can't be certain that you are not responsible." I knew my words did not comfort her, but she had to understand the gravity of the situation. We couldn't explain what happened in my father's chamber.

"Let me explain to your family, to anyone who needs to hear it," she continued.

"It would be a huge risk to expose who you are, knowing so little about you. If there is a trial, then everyone—not just my family—would know it too. I cannot fight everyone. We must leave."

"Where will we go?"

"I don't know, but someplace where I can keep you safe until I can sort this all out."

She finally conceded and began to pack.

Someone knocked on my door.

"Who is it?" I asked.

"It's me, Leo. Can I come in?"

So much had happened in so little time. Not even an hour ago I'd wanted to kill him, wanted to tear his throat out. Now he may be our ally. Maybe.

I opened the door, but only wide enough to ensure it was Leo.

"I am not here to hurt her. I only want to talk," said Leo. I believed him.

I opened the door all the way and let him inside. He glanced at Michaela but did not say a word to her.

"We need a story. We need to explain John's death," said Leo.

"Are you sure he's dead?" asked Michaela. Leo looked at her and nodded once.

"Say that I killed him," I told Leo. "He has enough bruises on his body to prove that I beat him to death. Say a final blow to his temple did him in. And make sure everyone knows why. I don't want the traitor to be pitied, I want him to be an example to anyone else who tries to kill the king—family or not."

"He did not have a trial," said Leo.

"It does not matter. Justice needed to be swift. He tried to kill me with that knife," I said.

"We don't know if he was aiming for you or Michaela," said Leo.

"I wasn't going to wait to find out," I sneered. "Regardless, an attempt to kill Michaela is the same as an attempt on my life."

Leo nodded. Then, "What about the family? How do we ensure Theodore stays quiet and goes along with this story?"

"I will talk to him, tell him that I am not finished with him. I will warn him to keep with this story. Otherwise, he will be investigated as an accomplice. In fact, I'm not too sure he isn't. I don't know if I buy John's explanation that he worked alone."

"I agree," said Leo. "Although I don't know if we will ever discover who his accomplice is, unless they try again."

I hadn't thought of that. I needed bodyguards around my father, ones I could trust. "Leo, I am sorry I accused you. I was angry and I couldn't see past my first thought. I didn't seek to understand, I just went with my baser instincts to attack."

Leo nodded again but didn't say anything.

"Can we get past this?" I asked.

"Yes," he finally responded, and I was relieved. "I probably would have done the same thing." He stretched out his hand and I proudly shook it.

"I need to get Michaela somewhere safe while I try to figure this all out. Can I trust you to watch over my father while I'm gone?"

"Of course, Hunter. I know we haven't always seen eye to eye, but you can count on me to be loyal to the king and to you."

"Thank you," I said, and this time I leaned in to pat his back, in what Laura would call a man hug.

I turned to Michaela. "I will go speak to my family now. I'll be back soon. Will you be ready to leave immediately when I return?"

"Yes, I won't be long," she said.

I grabbed her hands and leaned in to give her a kiss. "Everything is going to be all right," I reassured her and myself. Then, I left her packing and headed back to my father's chambers with Leo beside me.

Once inside, I noticed someone had removed John's body from the room, but Theodore and Elenora still remained. So did Aunt Olympia; she sat by my father's side.

"How is he?" I asked her.

"He seems to be improving. He opened his eyes a little while ago and called out your name," she said.

I walked over to the bed and noted that indeed my father's pallor had improved. He kept moving his lips, mumbling to himself. It sounded incoherent, but even this gave me hope that he would get better. She'd done it. I couldn't help but believe that Michaela had something to do with this.

"She is a powerful being," said Elenora, shrewd as always.

"Yes." I did not deny it.

"What is she?" she asked.

"I do not know," I lied. "I am going to take her away until we find out exactly what she is capable of. It appears she may be responsible for my father's improvement."

"And my son's death," Theodore growled.

I faced my uncle, infused as much strength as I could manage into my voice, and responded, "Your son tried to kill my father, his king. He got what he deserved. He got what our laws demand of traitors."

"I cannot deny what he did, as he admitted as much. However, it was not her place to be the executioner," my uncle said while pointing to the door Michaela had exited from earlier. "She is not one of us, never will be, and did not have any right to kill my son. She is a killer!" He shouted the last part, and I knew if I did not gain control right now, I would have to fight my uncle, as well.

"Do I need to remind you, Uncle," I said with all the authority of the heir to the throne, "that your son pulled a knife out to kill me—"

"No, he was aiming for her," he interjected.

"You don't know that for sure and neither do I. What I do know is that he admitted to treason and, from where I stood, attempted to kill the next in line to rule. I should have killed John myself, but Michaela stopped me. She saved your son, Uncle, but then he couldn't leave it alone."

His head shook violently from side to side. He still raged and would not listen or look at me as I spoke. I had to change tactics from defense to offense.

"Besides, Uncle, you should be more concerned about yourself," I said.

"Myself? What are you talking about?"

"I am not convinced that John acted alone. I believe he had help." I looked him straight in the eye. He shook his head again. But then looked at me.

"You cannot be insinuating that I colluded with him?" he responded, not backing away from my gaze. Our eyes continued to bore into each other for a few more seconds until I gave him one last warning.

"I suggest you follow my orders and do not give me any reason to doubt you," I said.

Theodore scrutinized me, but he didn't say a word. So much hate, rage, and restlessness raced through his body. I did not know if he would let this one go. I did not know if he would ever forgive Michaela for this, and a manticore as powerful as Theodore could not be dismissed. My instinct to get Michaela out of here was correct. I had to get back to my room and remove her from this place immediately.

There was one more thing I needed to make clear, however. "John's death will be an example of how this kingdom responds to traitors. As far as anyone is concerned, I killed John." I turned my head and looked around the room to ensure I had all of their attention.

"I should have been the one to kill John, not Michaela. When he came after us, she acted in self-defense. She did nothing wrong. The kingdom, however, will not know this version of events, as we need to keep her identity a secret until we understand more about her."

"I agree. She could be a powerful weapon," said Elenora cunningly.

Her words stopped me from leaving the room. I turned slowly toward my father's twin. "Michaela is not and never will be a weapon. Do you understand?"

"But she can ensure our family rules for at least another century," she countered. I continued to stare and said nothing until she conceded. "Fine. We will keep this a secret until we know more."

It was not the response I wanted, but it was as good as I would get from Elenora for now. It would not be easy to keep powerful manticores from wanting more power. That's why I had to get Michaela away before anyone else suspected what she was and what she could do. I started to think we'd only discovered the tip of the iceberg regarding her powers.

After I left the room, I dialed Laura's number. It took a while, but she finally answered. She sounded out of breath, "Hunter, hi. What's going on? Is Father all right?"

"Yes, in fact, he seems to be improving."

"That's great news," she said.

"Listen, Laura, I need to leave town for a few days," I said.

"Is everything okay?" she asked.

"It will be, and I promise to explain it all when I get back," I said. "But in the meantime, could you stay in the mansion with Father? I'd feel better if you were here and looking over the family while I'm gone. Leo is in charge of watching over Father, but I'd like you to be the one to liaison with the family. Call me if anything comes up that I need to be aware of."

"Of course, Hunter, no problem."

"Thanks. I need to call Thomas now and let him know I'll be leaving town. I need him to take care of business while I'm away."

"Oh, um, Thomas is here with me. I can tell him," she said.

"He is, is he? Put him on the phone." A smile spread across my face. I was glad neither of them could see it.

"Hello," said Thomas.

"Are you dating my sister?" I snarled at him.

"What? No, Hunter. I swear I'm not," he said. *Too bad.* "I don't know how much of that you heard, but I need you to take care of Durand Enterprise while I'm away. It will only be for a few days. I'll call you if it is longer."

"Don't worry about a thing,. I've got it under control."

"Thanks, Thomas. And take good care of my sister."

"I will," he said, this time not broaching any argument.

Finally, I could get back to Michaela and we could get the hell out of New York City.

Twenty-Nine

Michaela

Hunter rented a car when we arrived in Toronto. A song played on the radio, and I smiled to myself. It was one of Tricia's favorite songs to play in the office. It brought me back to a few short weeks ago when life was simpler. When I only had to worry if restaurants took reservations before dinner and if the barista used skim milk instead of almond milk in my coffee. I shook my head and wondered what I was so stressed about then. I hadn't appreciated how simple my life was. I'd only cared about the next event and reaching the next promotion. I was not the same person I was three weeks ago. I didn't know who I was now, or what I was supposed to do. How could I go back to my ordinary life when I knew of these extraordinary beings? How could I when I, too, may be one of them? How did I pretend nothing had happened? I may have killed someone and knew nothing of how I'd done it. What if I did it again, this time to an innocent person?

I looked over at Hunter. He drove in silence, his handsome face concentrating on the road ahead. He turned his head to look at me and concern framed his eyes.

"You're frowning," said Hunter. "What are you thinking about?"

"I'm scared," I admitted. "What if I hurt somebody else? What if this is who I am now?"

"Michaela, you are not a killer. Just because we suspect you may have abilities does not mean you are going to use them to hurt people. That's not you," he said in a soft voice. "Besides, I believe you and your abilities saved my father."

"But I did hurt someone," I replied. I couldn't get the image of John laying on the ground out of my head.

"You acted out of self-defense. If the roles were reversed and you were the one laying on the ground, John would not regret his actions." I nodded because he was right. I just had to remind myself that I hadn't intended to kill him.

"You're right. I need to get this entire ordeal out of my head. I need to go back to the way things were three weeks ago, when everything made sense."

He reached out and grabbed my hand over the stick shift.

"Well, maybe with one exception," I said and smiled. I straightened my spine, shrugged my shoulders, and attempted to shake off the weight of the last few days. I took a deep breath and exhaled.

"Are we headed to your apartment or to your aunt Julie's house?" asked Hunter.

"My apartment. I need to be alone," I said.

Hunter frowned. "I understand you needing some space, but I can't leave you alone in your apartment right now. We may be away from New York but we still don't know who the shooter was in Italy or what he wanted from us. He may still be out there."

I wanted Hunter with me, that's not what I had meant by alone. I just didn't want to explain what happened in New York to my aunt Julie tonight. I was exhausted and I needed to get some rest. So, I simply nodded.

"I do want to stop by your super's apartment, though, and have a word with him about getting new locks for your door."

"Of course. Do what you think is best. I know I need to forget about things for a little while."

"I don't want you to forget everything from the last few days," he said. He raised my hand and kissed the back of it. An image of the two of us in his bed came to mind.

Yes, some things, I never wanted to forget.

He pulled up to my apartment building and parked in one of the visitor's spots. "I'll walk you to your apartment before heading to the super's place," he said as he got out of the car.

"Oh, you don't have to do that, Hunter. I've lived on my own and walked myself to my door many times. I'll be fine," I said.

He blew out a breath and looked ready to argue but when I raised one of my eyebrows, he relented. "Keep your phone next to you."

"Yes, of course."

"All right, I won't be long."

"Take your time. I think I'm going to take a long, hot bath and soak there until I shrivel up."

He laughed and kissed me on the forehead. "Save some energy for dinner. I'll order us something special," he said.

"Sounds like a plan." This time he kissed my lips and let his mouth linger there. The kiss was soft and sweet, exactly what I needed.

"See you in a bit," I said and walked away.

I felt Hunter's eyes on me while I crossed the lobby. The white marble foyer in my building blanketed me with comfort as I walked toward the elevators. The girl who lived on the ninth floor stood in front of the doors when they opened, and we both walked inside.

"Hi, there," I said.

She didn't respond, but I heard music blasting from her earphones. Her gum popped in rhythm with the beat. I smiled. Even this familiar encounter that once would've annoyed me, gave me comfort.

Inside my apartment, everything was exactly as I'd left it. I didn't know why I had a sinking feeling that the place would be ransacked.

I guess I'd been imagining the worst. I had to let those negative feelings go and see the path ahead in a more positive light. I should focus on what I was most thankful for: my aunt Julie, Dev, meeting Veronica and Signora Tassone. And of course, there was Hunter. I was most thankful for him.

After I locked the door, I walked to my room and put my phone down on my bed. The screen lit up, and I realized I had a voicemail notification. I couldn't bear to be in these clothes any longer, so I put my phone on speaker and undressed.

"You have three unheard messages. First message," the voicemail service called out as I shook off my jacket.

"Mickey, it's Tricia. Call me when you're back. We have a huge new potential client we need to prepare for. It's big. Like Gucci big. Like Dior big. Like the Eiffel Tower big. Hope you had a good vacay. Bye."

I smiled because this sort of message would have angered me in the past, but now I was happy to be home and wanted to get back to work. I'd call her tomorrow, though.

"Next message," the voicemail intoned.

"Michaela, it's Dev. I hope you had a great vacation, can't wait to hear all about it. Ah, I missed you so much this week. Work was unbearable. Tricia was on a rampage about getting some presentation together and needed new bio pics. She insisted we color-coordinate and, of course, she chose the colors for everyone. You're to wear blue, by the way. I met someone at the coffee shop down the street the other day. I need to dissect every word and hand gesture with you, so call me when you get back. Miss you."

I grinned this time and picked up my cell phone to call Dev. I couldn't wait to dive into all the tiny details of that encounter.

"Next message." I waited for the last message to play.

"Michaela, ciao, it's Veronica. I hope you are okay. Please call me when you are back home. I would like to talk to you. Ciao."

I checked the time, it was nearly 11:00 p.m. in Italy. It would be too late to call Veronica now. I would call her first thing in the morning. I dialed Dev's number instead.

"Hello? Michaela, is that you?" Dev answered after just one ring.

"It's me!"

"Oh, I'm so happy you're back."

"Me too."

"How did it go?"

"Um, uneventful. Saw my grandparents' old village and met some of the locals. It was nice. Enough about me, tell me everything. Did he order a latte or a cappuccino?"

"Neither. It was an English Breakfast Tea."

"Oh, now you've really got my attention," I said, and he laughed on the other end. Dev's laugh turned into a snort and the outburst surprised me. He was always so prim and proper. I laughed at his slipup. A real, belly-aching laugh. I settled onto the couch and enjoyed the conversation with Dev.

Thirty

Michaela

I was asleep in the bathtub when a knock on the front door woke me. I reluctantly got out of the tub and dried off. The knock grew louder this time. I grabbed the robe hanging from my bathroom door and tied it tightly around my waist. I checked the peephole. Hunter stood on the other side staring toward the hallway.

When I opened the door, Hunter held up a paper bag and a box. "The driver just dropped off our dinner." He lifted the paper bag and I could smell the savoury aroma of something spicy and flavorful. "Penne Arriabbata with meatballs," he confirmed.

"Sounds perfect," I said.

He handed me the box and I groaned, "Chocolate covered strawberries are my favorite." He grinned at having chosen the right desert and I playfully slapped his arm.

"Let me put these in the fridge for later." I walked down the hallway to the kitchen and Hunter followed. I had just placed the strawberries on the refrigerator rack when Hunter grabbed my hip and spun me around. "I missed you," he growled and pulled me into his arms.

I laughed. "You were barely gone for thirty minutes."

Hunter wasn't laughing. His hand rubbed my back and then moved lower. "I hardly have enough control when you are fully clothed. You are killing me in this robe," he murmured.

"I won't lie, I like the power it gives me to see you at my mercy." I smiled and wrapped my arms around his neck.

"I am at your mercy. And I don't mind admitting that I enjoy the power you wield over my thoughts and my body. I enjoy the temptation, and when you give in to that temptation too," he said and placed both his hands on my hips and squeezed. "I love the struggle of power and pleasure between us," he whispered.

My heart raced after hearing his words. I enjoyed it too. I loved that we both wanted to be in control and relished when we relinquished it to each other. I had never given anyone else such power over me. I had only let my guard down with Hunter.

"I want you," I whispered as he pulled me in closer. "I don't know how much longer I can hold out. We need to find a way soon."

"I'm working on it. I have some ideas, but I want to check with Professor Wallace first," he said in between kisses to my neck and cheek.

"Good," I whispered and reached up to kiss him fully on the mouth.

The kiss began softly but changed into something more emotional. It felt like all our frustrations, fears, and love poured out of our mouths, filling each other's needs.

He untied my robe and I allowed it to fall off my shoulders. It pooled at my feet. Hunter took a step back. I thought he would walk away, but instead he stared at me.

"You are so beautiful," he said.

I didn't feel awkward standing there, or cold. I didn't rush to pick up my robe. I just stood and basked in the heat from his eyes. I thought I would be more self-conscious, but I wasn't. I felt strong and powerful. I felt like a goddess. I stepped forward to pull him against me when a buzzing sound stopped me.

Hunter looked annoyed and searched his pocket to find his phone. When he glanced down at his screen, he frowned.

"I don't recognize this number," he said, studying his phone.

"Oh, it's probably just Veronica. She tried to get ahold of me too."

Hunter tapped the screen to answer his phone. "Hello?"

I couldn't hear the voice on the other end, but I heard Hunter reply, "Yes, this is Hunter. Who is this?"

Hunter raised his eyes and looked at me. "Yes, she is here with me. But you haven't answered my question yet."

Another response I didn't hear, but Hunter clipped out a reply. "Fine," he said into the phone. Then to me, "He insists he only speak to you. I'll be right here, by your side." Then he handed me the phone.

Before I took it, I dropped to pick up my robe and put it on. A chill permeated the air now. I tied the robe tightly around me and stuck my hand out for the phone.

"Hello," I said.

"Is this Michaela Morrone?"

"Yes, who is this?"

"Are you the daughter of Lucia Shedley?" asked the voice on the other end.

"Yes. Again, who is this?"

I peeked up at Hunter. I suspected he could hear the other person's voice on the phone because he appeared to be concentrating rather than waiting for me to answer.

"My name is Nicholas Giannis. You do not know me, but I've been looking for you," he said.

"How did you get this number?" I asked but then remembered Hunter leaving his card with Signora Tassone.

"One of my men called me and said he had met a woman with violet eyes at a restaurant in southern Italy. Then word reached me that foreigners had visited Signora Tassone. I called her today to inquire who it was, and she reluctantly told me it was you, Lucia's daughter. I could not believe it. I cannot believe Lucia had a daughter. She never told anyone about you. It is a miracle," he said, and he sounded genuinely happy, but I was still not convinced.

"Are you the one she met with when she came to Italy? Are you my grandmother's fiancé?" I demanded.

"I see Signora Tassone told you about me. But I am not your grandmother's fiancé—that was my father. Oh, Michaela, I am so happy to have found you," he said.

His happiness angered me. Was he happy to learn of my existence because he'd lost his apprentice?

"My parents are dead because of you. For all I know, you could be the one responsible for their deaths," I accused him.

He did not respond right away, and I worried I may have said too much too soon. If he ended the call, I would never know the truth about my parents. I was about to tell him not to hang up when he responded very quietly. "I could never hurt your mother. How could I? She was our warrior, our healer, our only hope," he said reverently.

"If that's true, then why did someone take down her plane? Why did someone try to shoot me at the airport?" I shouted into the phone..

"We were not aiming to hurt you," he said. "Adam, my son, wasn't trying to shoot you, he was trying to shoot *him*."

I went cold.

"Him?" I repeated. "You mean Hunter?"

"Yes, that beast. That manticore," he ground out, as though he could not even spit the name out.

"Manti-what?" I asked, confused. Hunter raised his hand, about to grab the phone from me, but I turned my back away from him.

"What did you call him?" I asked, and when Hunter was in front of me again, I held my palm up toward him to hold him back.

"Has he not told you what he is?" Nicholas asked. "Has he kept his true identity a secret from you? Why do you think that is? He does not want you to know what he truly is, what he's capable of."

Images of Hunter gashing John's flesh with his teeth and roaring until I thought my ears would bleed flashed through my mind. My stomach dropped to my feet, and I thought I would throw up.

"He is a creature who lives in the shadows," continued Nicholas. "They are fueled by anger and ruled by their predator instincts. They are dangerous and unpredictable. They don't belong with humans."

I sank down to the floor and pressed my back against the kitchen cabinets to hold me up. When I still didn't respond, Nicholas continued. "Your mother knew this, Michaela, and she worked hard to help us."

"How did she help you?" I asked somberly.

"She was our leader. She sought manticores out, uprooted them from their hiding places and got rid of them," he explained. "My father taught her who she could be, and she was perfect. She was everything my father had dreamed your grandmother could be, but perhaps that wasn't in her stars. Perhaps the glory was to be your mother's, and now it could be yours."

"What are you talking about?" I asked.

"Michaela, you are a Shed woman. You are among the protectors of this earth, and The Sheds are one of the strongest. You heal, fight, and guard against creatures such as him."

"But Hunter is not like that," I tried to explain, but it sounded weak. My confusion muddled down my argument.

"He is one of their leaders, their heir," he said. "Has he kept that from you too?" I looked up at Hunter but his face revealed nothing to me. Nicholas lowered his voice and said, "We do not know where his kingdom is hidden but we suspect it is deep underground." While I had barely heard Nicholas's words Hunter must have had no trouble because his back stiffened. "He is one of the most powerful manticores in the kingdom."

I waited for Hunter to deny it, to deny any of it. But he said nothing, only stared at me.

"I am telling you this to warn you and make you understand that he's using you."

"No," I said and shook my head.

Nicholas sighed loudly, he sounded frustrated with my refusal to listen. "I hear his father is on the mend," he continued. "Was that your doing? Did you want to save him or did Hunter ask you to do it?

"I..." I started to explain that I'd wanted to save his father, that Hunter had never asked it of me, but I couldn't recall how it went. *Who was the first to suggest it?*

Instead, I said something I wasn't expecting to blurt out.

"I killed one of them," I whispered and then let out a sob.

"Don't cry, Michaela. It's what you are meant to be. You are light in their darkness. You were born to root out such evil. It is in your blood. I am proud of you. So proud," he said. "Come to me. Let us teach you all that you are capable of. Leave him and don't ever look back."

I peeked at Hunter, and he didn't say a word. Why wasn't he arguing back?

"Why should I believe you? Why should I believe any of this?" I asked. "I love him, and he loves me." But for the first time, doubt wormed its ugly head into my thoughts.

"He doesn't love you. He wants to possess you, wield your power, and use you as a weapon. He gives you what you want now because you have given him what he wants. You've healed his father. What happens when he asks you to do something you are not prepared to do? Kill someone you don't want to kill. Be that weapon he wants you to be? Your mother tried to listen to one of them, even befriended him but he betrayed her and had her killed."

"*What?*" I said, not wanting to believe, but wanting to know more.

"Manticores hunted her down and eventually found her. They shot down her plane. Your parents are dead because of them."

Hunter shook his head and waved his hand, denying it. Finally, a denial. But was it too late?

"I don't know what to think. I need time," I heard myself say. "How can I reach you?"

"I've given Veronica my number. I've never left them with contact information before, but when she could not get ahold of you, I became desperate to finally reach you. You can contact me through her."

"Okay. I will want more information, more of an explanation, but not tonight. I cannot handle any more revelations tonight," I said, holding Hunter's phone against my ear and my head with the other hand.

I ended the call and sat on my kitchen floor. I was broken. My whole world turned upside down. The conversation incited a vertigo that left me paralyzed on the floor.

"Michaela," Hunter said, crouching beside me. "Come sit on the couch. You don't look well."

He tried to lift me, but I pulled my arm back. I didn't want to move. I thought I may be sick if I moved even an inch.

"I want you to deny it. Deny it all," I said.

"I cannot deny it all," he whispered.

"Why didn't you tell me what you are? Why do I have to hear it from some stranger in God knows what country?"

"You knew I could not tell you everything," he explained.

"I knew there was this secret between us," I said, and an awful thought popped into my head. "Yes, I knew, and how convenient of you to throw that back in my face," I shouted. "I trusted you. I was patient with you but you continued to keep me in the dark. Were you really worried about your family using me as a weapon, or did you want to keep me and my abilities all to yourself?"

"I do want to keep you all to myself, but not as a weapon, as my partner, as my lover," he said.

"Lover? Really? Are you worried about us being together because perhaps I could hurt you and not the other way around? Has this always been about you and not me? Are you afraid of what I could do to you?"

"Yes, you could break my heart without even trying, but that's not why," he said and straightened himself up. He paced the room. His hands curled into fists, opened, and curled again. He looked like he was fighting with himself.

"Dammit," he said and looked to the ceiling. "The only way to gain your trust again is to tell you things I am not permitted to say." He did not face me but he continued talking. "Manticores cannot be with humans. The poison that runs in our veins would kill you."

"What if I'm not all human?" I asked.

"Exactly, and that's what I'm trying to find out." He turned toward me, pleading with his eyes.

Mine had turned cold. I'd heard too much that had me questioning my every move, his every motive.

"Is it true?" I forced myself to ask about what would be the worst betrayal of all.

"Is what true?" he asked.

"The part about my parents. Were they killed by..." I couldn't finish the sentence.

"No, I don't think so. I've never heard of this, and I would have known of such an order," he said, but he didn't sound convinced. Was he telling me the truth? I didn't know what to believe anymore.

"I need some time to process everything," I said.

He nodded his head. "I understand. I'll leave you alone tonight and we can talk in the morning." He approached to help me up.

"No, you don't understand what I'm saying, Hunter." I held my head in my arms, but then I looked up and stared at him straight in his amber eyes.

"I don't want you to come back in the morning. I don't want you to come back...for a while. I need some time to sort this all out in my head. I need to meet with Nicholas and understand what he's telling me. I need to decide for myself whom to trust."

"You can trust me," he said fervently.

"I don't know for sure that I can," I said solemnly.

"How can you say that?"

I remembered sitting in Hunter's car on our first date. He'd told me he didn't want to pursue a long-distance romance. He'd only come back to me when he thought I could save his father. Then on the way to the airport in Italy, he'd said he couldn't introduce me to his family. We hadn't found anything that could save his father in Italy, and he was prepared to let me go and return to Toronto alone. Only his conscience had made him bring me to New York. I couldn't help these dangerous thoughts. *Is that really the truth? Have I built up this romance in my head?*

"All I can say is that nothing is as it was three weeks ago. The world is not as it seems. Family, life, death—all have new implications for me, and I need time to sort it all out."

"How much time?" he asked. His jaw ticked from holding back his emotions. I didn't know if it was anger or frustration.

I shook my head. "I don't know. But I can't think when you're here."

"I don't trust that man. I don't trust that he won't hurt you. I don't want you meeting with him."

I raised my eyebrows at this. I felt the goddess in me return and perhaps the warrior Nicholas said I was meant to be. I'd never liked to take orders from anyone.

"Well, that's too bad," I said. "The time for you to have asserted yourself was ten minutes ago when he accused you of using me," I shouted at him.

"How can you believe that? I didn't think I needed to defend that. I thought you understood how much I love you, that you felt the same. But perhaps yours was just a fleeting feeling."

"Yes, I needed you to deny it then. I still need to hear the words now," I countered.

He straightened and stared at me. "I did not and never would use you, Michaela. I have only ever wanted to protect you, even when it was from myself."

"What are you talking about?"

"When I let you go back to Toronto the first time, it was because I was too afraid of being close to you and losing control, of hurting you. I knew how hard it would be to hold you and not want to lay you down. So, I strengthened my resolve to protect you. I let you go."

"That's why you didn't want to see me again?" I asked.

He nodded.

"Well, I guess this time, I will have to let you go," I said and knew what I needed to do. "I have to find out who I really am and where my family comes from. Only then can I decide how I want to move forward."

Hunter ran his fingers through his hair and paced my apartment. After several minutes he dropped down to his knees in front of me. He lifted up my chin with his fingertips and I stared into his amber eyes. "Go, then. Go find yourself, Michaela. Because when you do, I'll be right here waiting."

His words made me shiver. They were exactly what I wanted to hear, but I couldn't help but wonder if there was a warning in them.

"Goodbye, Hunter," I said.

"Goodbye, Michaela."

And with those last words, he turned and left me sitting in my apartment alone. Scared, confused, heartbroken, and lost. But I'd been here before. I was a fighter, a survivor, a warrior. I'd always picked myself up. No matter how many times life had brought me to my knees, I always stood right back up. This time wouldn't be any different. I sat there in my kitchen a little bit longer, though.

Thirty-One

Hunter

The flight back to New York was excruciating. I hadn't slept the night before. I had replayed what happened in Michaela's apartment over and over in my mind, wondering if there was anything I could have done differently. I could not deny that I was a manticore; I would not lie to her like that. I could not deny we were powered by our predator instincts. I could not even deny that we had a hidden kingdom. *How the hell did this guy know so much?*

But the part that haunted me the most was the betrayed look on Michaela's face. I'd betrayed her, and I felt responsible for that look. I hadn't lied, but I hadn't been honest with her either. I couldn't explain that to her; I was hardly comforted by the semantics of it.

On the drive back to my father's house, I came up with a plan. The best way to get Michaela back was to find out who really killed her parents. Once she knew the facts about what had happened, she would trust me and know that I would always tell her the truth.

I called ahead and asked Leo, Laura, Thomas, and James to meet me at my father's house. I needed help uncovering this plot.

As soon as I arrived, I walked straight to my father's chambers. Leo and the physician were there with him.

"How is he?" I asked.

"Oh, Hunter, welcome back," said the physician, obviously missing the impatience in my voice.

"Thank you. How is my father?" I asked again.

"Hunter," a low but strong voice called my name. I immediately recognized it to be my father's.

"Father, you can speak," I said, rushing to his bedside.

"Yes," he said. "Getting stronger every day."

"Yes, that is true," said the physician. "Your father's health is improving. It progressed slowly at first, but he is talking more today. His heart and lungs are strong. I expect him to make a full recovery."

"This is great news," I said.

"Indeed," said the king. "I understand I have someone to thank for it."

"Well, we cannot be sure that my remedies did not work," said the physician, clearly not wanting to give credit to another source. "But of course, prayer is always a welcome addition to medicine."

My father looked up at me and smiled. He knew when not to argue; it had always been his strong suit with my mother.

When the physician left the room, I placed my hand on top of my father's and said, "I am glad you are recovering. When you feel better, there's much I'd like to discuss with you." I didn't want to exhaust him with all my questions, but I hoped soon he would be strong enough to endure them.

"Yes, Hunter, we will talk very soon," he promised and closed his eyes.

I left him to rest and motioned Leo outside.

"Welcome back," he said as we headed to the dining room where the others would meet us.

"Thank you. How have things been here?" I asked.

"Quiet. Which is good. Not much has happened. We did what you told us to do, and the kingdom seems to be responding well to how the situation with John was handled. I think it may have been the perfect balance to your father's act of mercy."

"Good," I said, glad at least that was working out.

When we arrived inside the dining room, Laura, Thomas, and James were already sitting at the table.

"Hunter, nice of you to call a meeting in a dining room with no food," said Laura, the consummate host.

A smile tugged on my lips, and I poured her a drink. "Who needs food when there's whiskey," I said. She accepted the glass with a smile.

"So, why have you called us all here? Is it about the king?" asked James.

"Not in the context you're thinking," I said. "Father is on the mend, and I hope to ask him some questions when he's feeling better. For now, I asked you all here because last night, I received a call from some man named Nicholas Giannis." I paused to see if that name sounded familiar to anyone. As I suspected, no one reacted, so I continued. "He didn't want to speak to me, however. He wanted to talk to Michaela. He told her what we are," I said.

"What!" shouted Thomas. "But how does he know?"

"I don't know. In fact, he knows a lot about us. He even knows there is a secret kingdom hidden somewhere, but says he doesn't know where it is. The fact that he even knows it exists worries me."

"Exactly," said James.

"Do you want us to hunt him down?" asked Leo.

"No, not yet," I explained. "Michaela was really shaken up by the things he told her."

"I can imagine," said Laura. "Poor girl."

"Well, she doesn't need our pity, she needs our help," I went on. "She understandably is confused right now. She doesn't trust us."

"Why not?" asked Leo.

"Because this man told her we are predators," I explained. "And that we are responsible for her parents' death."

The room was silent. And then, Laura spoke up. "Are we? I mean, did a manticore kill her parents?"

"I don't know. I don't recall it, and I think I would have heard if a manticore had killed two humans, wouldn't I? That's why I need to question Father. But not yet. Not until he's stronger."

"What else did this man say?" asked Leo. He always had a way of knowing when there was more to a story.

"He told Michaela she is a warrior. Someone who hunts down manticores."

"You mean, she is our enemy?" asked Leo.

"No, of course not. But this man, he wants to turn her into some manticore slayer. It's not who she is."

"Well, she did kill John," Leo added.

"John deserved to die. She just beat me to it."

"Hunter," said James, but I interrupted him because I needed to make this point clear.

"Michaela is not our enemy. She is just confused right now and needs time to sort it all out. If I can find out what really happened to her parents, then I think I can gain her trust once again. I think she will understand we are not the monsters Nicholas portrays us to be."

"Hunter," said James again.

"Yes, James, was it?" I asked.

"I remember where I saw her eyes before," he said.

"What are you talking about?" I asked.

"Remember the first day I met her, back in my apartment for that magazine interview?" he explained.

I tried to recall that day, but the only thing I remembered was losing control of my instincts and kissing her for the first time.

I remembered the kiss having an effect on James's heart and mine. But not Leo's. But Leo rarely paid attention to anything when there were attractive females around. Could Michaela's fear of being caught have caused mine and James's hearts to stop for a second?

Hmm, I needed to discuss this with Professor Wallace. "Are you referring to what you said about your heart?" I asked James.

"Yes and no. I am still curious about that. But I said that I had seen her eyes before, and you agreed that maybe you had too."

Yes, I did recall saying that.

"I think I remember now where I saw them before," he said.

"Where?" I asked.

"In your father's study."

He dropped this bomb and it exploded in my head.

"What are you talking about? Michaela has never been in my father's study." I couldn't comprehend what he was talking about.

"No, that's not what I meant," he clarified. "This was a couple decades ago, I believe. I recall waiting in your father's study for you, while you were getting ready for us to leave town for a bit. It was a trip to celebrate your birthday. There was a photo of a woman on his desk. I remember being drawn to it because she was extremely beautiful. The woman had the most unusual eyes—violet like Michaela's. In fact, they looked identical to hers. I think the photo was of her mother."

I processed the implications of this. Why would my father have a photo of Michaela's mother on his desk? What did he know of The Sheds?

"Do you think my father had anything to do with the death of her parents?" I asked, horrified. "If that's true, it would be over between us."

"I don't know," said James, shaking his head, and he then looked me straight in the eyes. "I do know, however, that this is far from over."

VIOLET SKY
Second Chances

DON'T MISS THE FINALE OF

MICHAELA & HUNTER'S STORY

AVAILABLE SEPTEMBER 2021

ACKNOWLEDGEMENT

A huge thank you to:

My husband and children, who supported this dream from the beginning.

To my alpha readers, Gilda and Lauren, who fell in love with my hero as much as I did and encouraged me to publish.

To my critique partners, Sam, Anuja, Nita, Jayme and Nadja, thank you for asking the hard questions and pulling me up to the next level.

To my editor, Katie, for her sharp eyes and mind.

To my cover designer Beti Bup, for their patience.

To Chantel Guertin, thank you for turning around and lending a hand to a novice author like me. Your support and generous spirit humbles me.

To the Facebook group 20booksto50k who made me believe that this crazy dream of mine was possible.

About the Author

Eve Marian is a former journalist and public relations executive. She lives in a suburb of Toronto with her husband, two children and clever cat named Chase.

To receive the latest information on new releases, giveaways, promotions and more, sign up for her newsletter at www.evemarian.com.

www.ingramcontent.com/pod-product-compliance
Lightning Source LLC
Chambersburg PA
CBHW030339310726
48979CB00001B/96

* 9 7 8 1 7 7 7 8 0 1 3 2 8 *